William Kinread is a solicitor
and company director. He lives
in North Yorkshire with his
wife, son and dog.

Also by William Kinread
Luger.

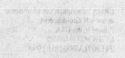

ESCAPEMENT

WILLIAM KINREAD

Fisher King Publishing

ESCAPEMENT

Print ISBN 978-1-914560-31-6

Digital ISBN 978-1-914560-34-7

Published by
Fisher King Publishing

www.fisherkingpublishing.co.uk

To my sister Anthea.

Escapement

Definition:

1. A mechanism consisting of an escape wheel and anchor used in timepieces to provide periodic impulses to the pendulum or balance.
2. An act or means of escaping.

Chapter One

June 1963 – Berlin

Separation hurts. Be it parent from child, a broken friendship or a parting of lovers, it twists the stomach and can break the heart. It can be caused by death, by betrayal, by deception. It can be a matter of geography or brought about by political will. Sin separates and hope lies in being reunited.

Theodor Hoffmann was running and was out of breath as he raced into the garage where his fiancée Angelika Jaeger and a childhood friend Frank Schafer were waiting for him.

'You should have heard him,' he said coming up behind Angelika and putting his arms around her waist. He kissed the top of her head and faced Schafer. 'I listened on the radio. He said, "in the world of freedom, the proudest boast is Ich bin ein Berliner," and we represent that fight for freedom.'

'You're such a dreamer Theo,' Schafer said, 'it must be your Italian blood.'

'Tyrolean,' Theo replied. He was proud of his late

father's heritage.

Angelika said nothing and broke away from his grip.

'Aren't you excited?' Theo asked.

'She's worried,' Schafer replied. 'This adventure is not without risk.'

'Yes, but we have to lift our eyes beyond the dangers of today, to the hopes of tomorrow,' Theo said regurgitating more of President Kennedy's speech.

Schafer walked over to the black Citroen DS. 'Okay, let's get on with it shall we?'

He flipped open the boot and placed Angelika's suitcase in the centre. It was a cream colour with brown leather trimmings. Then he placed a small matching make-up case to the side. Theo threw in his cheap black holdall to the right of both.

Schafer then opened a back door. He had removed the rear bench seat and created a plywood frame over which the seat covering was draped. There would be just enough room for Theo to lie on his side with his knees bent.

'No room for padding, I'm afraid but at least the Citroen has hydropneumatics suspension so you shouldn't be too uncomfortable,' Schafer said, smiling at Theo.

'Well, we don't have far to go,' Theo replied confidently.

Schafer handed Angelika a false passport showing she was a US citizen and a visa which stated she worked at the American embassy and had permission to enter East Berlin to visit relatives.

'Thanks Schafer,' Theo said handing him 10,000 Marks. Schafer peeled off 2,000 and handed them back.

'Here, I don't want to make a profit out of an old school friend and, in any case, the car is stolen. I thought the ambassadorial look might make you look more official. Now give me a hug and piss off!'

They embraced and Theo was about to get into position when he paused and pulled a deck watch out of his pocket wrapped in a soft cloth. It had been sent to his mother by his father just before he died. It looked like a pocket watch but was larger. Made by Lange & Sohne, it was silver with Arabic numerals and two subsidiary dials in the three and nine positions; one indicating the seconds and the other the power reserve. It was a well-made precision instrument used for telling the time on a ship's deck (after having been synchronised with a marine chronometer kept below decks). It had a swastika stamped on the back. He passed it to Angelika.

'Look after this for me, will you? It will stick into me if I lie on my side.' Schafer raised his eyebrows and Angelika slipped the watch into her handbag still saying nothing. Theo went to kiss her on the lips but she turned her face slightly. It was like she was frozen in time.

'I love you,' he said. She didn't reply.

Theo curled himself into position and Schafer wrapped the seat cover around the wooden frame.

'Good luck,' he said as he closed the door.

Angelika drove the Citroen carefully towards Checkpoint Charlie. It was a lovely warm summer's day and it was humid, which was important. Her long blonde, gently curled hair cascaded over her shoulders and her white blouse was unbuttoned just enough to reveal a small amount of cleavage. Her skirt was just above the knee, her legs were bare and she wore black court shoes with a medium heel. Her handbag and a dark grey jacket, matching her skirt, lay on the passenger seat next to her. The impression she gave was of a smart business woman; attractive and chic. Not tarty but sexy enough to raise the guard's interest.

Theo was sweating, finding it difficult to breathe under the back seat and the ride was uncomfortable, despite the Citroen's suspension. He had met Angelika three years ago at Humboldt University and, for him, it was love at first sight. She read law, he read languages and now they had graduated the time was right to make a break for freedom. It dominated his thoughts but Angelika wanted it too. For him it was a theoretical concept; he had felt trapped ever since the border with West Berlin was closed in 1961, but for Angelika it was raw ambition. She was determined to succeed in a way which was simply impossible under the communist system. Now, though, he was anxious. Throughout the planning stage he had always assumed that their escape would be successful but what if something went wrong? He didn't want Angelika to be in danger.

Angelika stopped at the barrier and a guard meandered out of his office. It was 3pm and he was hot and lethargic. That was part of the plan. They wanted people to be disinterested.

'Papers,' the guard grunted, wiping his forehead with a handkerchief.

Angelika handed over her passport and visa saying nothing but giving a pleasant smile. The guard opened her passport and then looked at her and noticed she was attractive.

'American?'

'Yes.'

'Purpose of visit?'

'Visiting my grandmother.'

'You don't sound American.'

'My parents are German. They emigrated before the War but returned afterwards to work at the World Health Organisation so I was brought up in Switzerland.'

The guard shrugged. It was neither approval nor disapproval.

'Is the boot open?'

'Yes,' Angelika replied.

The guard walked round to the back of the car, lifted the lid of the boot, saw the contents and shut the lid.

'Okay,' he said waving her on but then something gave him second thoughts. The cases didn't match. Two were feminine and the holdall was masculine.

Angelika just had 100 metres to drive, across what became known as the death strip, before she would reach the border. She pulled away slowly but the guard ran up to the driver's window and slapped it.

'Halt,' he shouted.

Angelika pushed the accelerator to the floor. The guard knelt on one knee and sprayed the back of the car with bullets from his machine gun. The nearside tyre burst and the Citroen swerved to the left and hit the kerb. Angelika grabbed her handbag and jumped out of the car. She only had thirty or so metres to go. She threw off her shoes and started running. She could cover the distance in a matter of seconds but there was still time for the guard to take a shot. He took aim at the centre of her back and was just about to fire when his superior officer who had run out of the guardhouse pushed the gun up in the air.

'No,' he said. 'Leave her. Let's check the car.'

Theo remembered the bright sunlight as the cover was pulled away from him, the order to get out shouted by the guard and Angelika staring at him from the safety of the West as he crawled out of the Citroen. Then he felt the impact of the rifle butt as it hit the back of his neck, just below the base of his skull. He must have been knocked unconscious because the next thing he remembered was being handcuffed, blindfolded and bundled into the back of a car. He had that strange feeling of lost time as the car rattled along the cobbled streets of Berlin.

The journey took about half an hour in his estimation until they arrived at an area not detailed on local maps. Even Western maps showed it as a blank space in Hohenschonhausen in the sub-district of Lichtenburg. To the local residents it was simply known as the Forbidden Area.

Theo was stripped and dressed in prison fatigues. Then he was taken along a corridor to an interrogation room with dark brick walls and a stone floor. There was a window but a guard manhandled him on to a small stool in front of a table with an empty chair opposite and he was too far from the window to see the view outside. He had no idea where he was.

Theo smelt him first. That foul smell of tobacco but mixed with garlic. Peter Schulz entered the interrogation room smoking, his uniform revealing that he was an officer in the notorious Stasi secret police. His hair was black and greasy.

Schulz pulled a Beretta from his holster and inspected it. He wore spectacles with a black frame, he was of medium height but over-weight and he wore black leather gloves. He sat down in the chair and pushed the gun against Theo's forehead, right between the eyes. Then he pulled the trigger. Theo must have closed his eyes at the last minute because all he could remember was the click of the action.

'Oh, dear. I must have forgotten to load it.' Schulz

laughed out loud as though he had been foolish. 'No matter. It makes no difference to me if you live or die. If you tell me what I want to know you may live, if not you will die. Do you understand Herr Hoffmann?'

'Yes,' Theo replied, realising that for him the psychological nightmare of Stasi interrogation had just begun. For some reason though he wasn't afraid. Not yet anyway. He was still taking everything in and the seriousness of his situation was offset by his knowledge that Angelika was safe.

Theo had dark ginger hair, cut short to calm the curls and he was of a similar size to Schulz but not as podgy. He was also a good ten years younger. Subconsciously, he must have been sizing Schulz up and coming to the conclusion that he was not that frightening but just a bully and like all bullies, a coward. However, he was not allowing for the fact that Schulz held all the cards.

Schulz put his gun back in its holster. 'Your attempted escape was with Angelika Jaeger. Where did she get her papers from?'

'Go to hell.' Theo said, surprising himself with his own bravado. He was protective of Angelika and he was taken off guard as he had expected some more basic questions first. He had not been long in captivity but clearly the Stasi had already started their investigations.

Schulz smiled, lent on the desk and pushed himself up slowly. He put his hands on his hips and then with one quick movement brought his left fist across Theo's left cheek. Theo's lip split and blood splashed out of the side of his mouth. Before he could recover, Schulz thumped him again with his right fist in the same place knocking Theo off the stool. The guard lifted him up and repositioned him. Theo was dazed and his body felt like jelly.

'I will make this easy for you Herr Hoffmann,' Schulz paused whilst he lit another cigarette, took a laboured drag and exhaled. 'You will tell me everything I want to know; it is just a matter of time and how much pain you would like to endure in the meantime. Goodnight.'

Schulz left the interrogation room and Theo was transferred to an isolation cell with a bed and a toilet. He wasn't sure of the time but Schulz had said "goodnight" so it must be evening. There were bright lights in the cell and no switches. Theo sat on the narrow wooden bed which had a two-inch mattress, a grey blanket and a pillow with no pillow case. Suddenly, he felt thirsty but there was no water. Then loud music started playing with a pounding regular beat.

Theo was puzzled as to why the interview had ended so abruptly. He lay on the bed and contemplated Schulz's words. He accepted that they would crack him; that everyone cracked eventually and there was no need to delay the flow of information as Angelika was safe. But he had to make it believable. What he had to do was give them the information they thought they wanted whilst not revealing his real secret and that meant he would have to suffer more pain. Both physical and psychological. The thought of that made him feel sick.

After several hours the lights went out and the music stopped. He fell asleep. It was late evening. The lights came back on and he was brought some breakfast of cold scrambled eggs. He had a splitting headache. This was all part of the disorientation process. There was virtually no natural light as the cell had only a narrow, frosted glass window just below the ceiling. He was being led to believe it was the morning of the next day when, in fact, it was the same night. There was nothing however by which he could ascertain the time.

Later he was briefly examined by a doctor and then a female guard led him back to the interrogation room and checked his name, address and date of birth. There seemed little reason to resist so he confirmed the details.

Schulz came back in and paced around him. 'We've found the owner of the stolen car. You may have changed the number plates but there are not many black Citroens in Berlin. The French government is not happy that it's riddled with bullets. Did you steal it?'

'No.' Theo had responded instinctively, denying the accusation but he did wonder if he should have given a different answer.

'So where did you get it?'

'From a man in a cafe.'

'What was his name?'

'I don't know.'

'Oh dear. You are slow to learn, Herr Hoffmann,' Schulz said as he suddenly stopped and smashed him across the left cheek again. 'And you're hurting my fist.'

Theo fell to the floor and Schulz kicked him in that soft part of the back which housed the kidneys. Theo arched his back in pain. Schulz stepped over him and kicked him under the chin. Theo felt his lower teeth crash into the upper and as a crimson pool of blood formed on the stone floor, he saw chips of white enamel floating on the surface.

Schulz left the room and Theo was transferred back to his cell. He did not know what time it was. He thought it was early morning but he was tired and his head hurt. He ran his tongue along the inside of his upper row of teeth and felt the rough chipped edges. He lay on the bed. He wanted to go to sleep but the lights were on and the music was blasting out of speakers above the door.

As he stared at the ceiling, Theo tried to come up with a strategy. If Schulz asked a question to which he already knew the answer, Theo would co-operate but if Schulz got too close, he would be evasive.

After eight hours of bright lights and loud music, Theo was exhausted. His head was throbbing and his ears ringing. Then the music stopped and a guard brought him a meal and some water. It was a horse meat stew with potato dumplings. Again, it was cold. He got the impression it was evening but it was actually late afternoon.

'Let's start again, shall we?' Schulz's demeanour was almost friendly, as though they were two colleagues that had got off on the wrong foot.

'You have just graduated from Humboldt University where for the last three years you have dated Angelika Jaeger to whom you are now engaged?'

'Yes,' Theo replied slowly whilst he calculated it was okay to confirm this. The Stasi were obviously making good use of his time in the cell to do their research.

'Do you know she has another lover?'

'That's a lie!' Theo came back fast and furious. He hadn't even slept with her. They were waiting until they were married. She was pure and innocent, like an angel; at least, that is how he saw her.

'I almost wish it was, for your sake,' Schulz sighed, as he walked behind Theo and stroked his shoulder. 'Personally, I prefer men. Far less complicated.' Theo shuffled uncomfortably on his stool. 'Tell me, does the name Aidan O'Sullivan mean anything to you?'

Theo stopped to think. He was an Irish lecturer at the Free University on the West side of the Wall but he had been allowed to visit Humboldt University to give the occasional lecture in public international law. Angelika had mentioned him in passing and been impressed by his intellect, but that was all.

'I've heard of him,' Theo replied.

'He is the man who's stolen her from you.'

'That's ridiculous. He's way older than Angelika and he's married with two daughters. She would never have anything to do with him,' Theo countered, spitting out the words.

'She's told you quite a lot about him then?'

'Get lost,' Theo said angrily. He had heard about the Stasi interrogation techniques of disorientation and disinformation but he feared he had just earned himself another beating. Instead, Schulz just walked to the door. He turned his head just before he disappeared.

'You've been deceived Herr Hoffmann. Think about that before our next meeting.'

Back in his cell the lights started flashing and the music seemed louder or, perhaps, just more unbearable. Theo's head felt it was about to explode. He just wanted to curl up in the corner and die. In fact, he did sit on the floor in the corner of the cell and put his face in the pillow to shield his eyes and protect his ears. It seemed to go on for hours. Then a guard burst in, pulled the pillow away from him and started kicking him. Theo was unable to protect himself and as he lay on the floor, he saw the jackboots swinging towards him again and again. He lay gasping for breath, bleeding. One of his eyes felt funny because the retina had become detached and his vision was blurred. Then he was dragged by his collar back into the interrogation room.

'You look a bit dishevelled, Herr Hoffmann. We shall

have to clean you up before your mother sees you.'

Theo had slumped his head on the table but now through blood blurred vision he looked up at Schulz.

'There will be a quick trial and you will go to prison for a couple of years. Your mother can come to court and say you are a good boy but impressionable. It would be a shame to keep such an intelligent young man locked up and she is sure you will contribute to society after some corrective training. Alternatively, she could lose her job, be evicted from her home and you can linger in prison unable to help her. Your choice Herr Hoffmann.'

Theo let his head slump back on the table. Schulz had won. He couldn't hold on any longer. He couldn't let them harm his mother. He raised his head perhaps just an inch.

'What do you want to know?'

'I want to know where you got the car and who gave you the false papers.'

'Schafer,' Theo mumbled. 'I got them from Schafer.'

'What's his full name?'

'I don't know. He's just known as Schafer – the Shepherd. I don't even know if it's his real name,' he lied.

'And you met him in a cafe?'

'He operates out of the Press Café in the Friedrichstrasse.'

'How much did you pay him?'

'10,000 Marks.'

'How old is Schafer?'

'About my age.'

'What does he look like?'

'Brown hair, a bit shorter than me.'

The questions kept coming quickly, one after another, and Theo answered them instantaneously which made his replies all the more convincing but all he actually gave away was vague details and the impression that "Schafer" was a nickname. He did not reveal Schafer's full name or address or the fact that they were childhood friends.

Eventually, after Schulz thought he had squeezed everything out of him, Theo was transferred to hospital for treatment to his eye and then to the Volkspolizei to await trial. As he was led out of the Stasi interrogation custody centre, he blinked in the sunlight with his one good eye. He had suffered more than he ever feared but he had survived. He had held on to his secret and, at least, Angelika would be safe in the embrace of the West. If he knew she was also in the embrace of another man he would not be so relieved.

Chapter Two

November 1989 – Harrogate

Ian's phone rang and Sarah, the receptionist, said Angela Jaeger had arrived for her appointment. Ian knew nothing about her, nor why she had made the appointment other than she had specifically asked for him. Normally Sarah would elicit some background information, but Angela's responses had been guarded.

'How do you do? I'm Ian Sutherland.' Ian held out his hand and received a firm handshake in response. That was good but it was almost too firm. It said, "I may be a woman but I'm as good as a man."

'Angela Jaeger. How do you do?'

So, she knows the etiquette, Ian thought although there was a strange mix in her accent. She was an attractive woman in her late forties, with blue eyes and shoulder length blonde hair. She wore a lilac V-necked sweater with no blouse underneath as her neck was bare, apart from a small silver necklace. She was slim and tight dark blue denim jeans and brown boots completed the outfit.

'Come on through,' Ian said as he led the way to one of

the interview rooms and held out a chair for her.

'Coffee?'

'Yes please,' Angela replied as she looked around and took in her surroundings. The room was as she expected. Like an old fashioned gentleman's club; dated but somehow reassuring.

Ian picked up the telephone and called reception. 'Two coffees please Sarah.'

'Now how can I help you?'

Angela eyed him up carefully. He was just as she had imagined. Tall, physically strong and immaculately dressed in a dark blue suit.

'I was born in Berlin but in 1963 I escaped and moved to Ireland.'

'Wow! That's interesting,' Ian replied with genuine curiosity.

That explained her accent. Her English was good but there was a slight clipped emphasis on some words mixed with the occasional Irish lilt.

'I have a law degree but I went into business. Caravan parks located at sailing centres. The business is very successful,' she said, pausing to let the information sink in. 'There is a high margin on caravans and we make customers buy a new one from us every ten years. We also get the ground rents and have a convenience store on every site.'

'How many sites do you have?' Ian asked.

'Three, near Dublin, Wexford and Cork.'

Ian waited for her to continue but she seemed slightly nervous.

'How did you hear about me? I understand you asked for me specifically?'

'Yes, I read about you in the paper.' She paused again and Ian, whilst flattered, started getting a little impatient.

'You will appreciate I can't practice Irish law. Are you wanting to expand the business into England?'

'No. I am hoping you will to go to Berlin for me and try to find someone.'

Ian took a sharp intake of breath. It was less than two weeks since the fall of the Berlin Wall and it was still dominating the news headlines with pictures of revelling students hacking away at the concrete with sledgehammers and pickaxes. It was a momentous event but Ian never thought in his wildest dreams that he would somehow become wrapped up in it.

'I'm afraid that's not the sort of thing we do. I'm basically a private client lawyer. If you wanted to buy a caravan park in England, I could help you but it sounds as if you need a private detective not a lawyer.' He sat back in his chair, almost giving a case closed posture.

'My escape in 1963 was attempted with my fiancé,' Angela said lowering her voice. 'He got caught but I made it across the border. He will have been interrogated by the Stasi and probably went to prison. I hope he is still alive but I have never had any contact with him since. Now I need to know what happened.'

'Couldn't you have written to him?' Ian asked.

'At first, I couldn't bring myself to do it. You see I was about to break off our relationship. He wanted marriage and children and I wanted a career. He was desperate to escape, though, so I was waiting until we were in the West before breaking the news to him. I thought that might lessen the blow. Then he got caught and I only had his mother's address. I didn't want to give away my location or give the Stasi anything else to work with.'

'I see,' Ian said and then 'thank you,' as Sarah brought in a cafetiere of fresh coffee and two cups and saucers. 'Please continue.'

'After a couple of years, though, I did write to him to say I had found a safe haven and settled down but I felt it was better for him if I released him from our engagement. However, I didn't say where I had settled or give any contact address. I didn't want the authorities to know where I was. I know this may sound a little silly to you but when you have lived under the watchful eye of the secret police you become a little paranoid.'

Ian nodded as he tried to process the information and passed her a cup of coffee.

'There's something else.' Angela was almost whispering now and looking down at the table. 'I was also in a relationship with another man. He is now my husband,

Aidan O'Sullivan, but I've kept my name for business purposes. We only got married nine years ago, when my daughter was born but we've lived together since 1963.'

'What was your fiancé called?' Ian asked, trying to fill the gaps in the story.

'Theo Hoffmann.'

'And does he know about Aidan O'Sullivan?'

'No.'

'And you want me to find him?'

'Yes. I want you to find him and tell him that I'm sorry that his dreams never came true. I would like you to tell him that I am willing to set him up financially in a location of his choice so at least his dream of freedom can be realised. I would like you to tell him that I would like to see him again, even if it is only once, just to explain everything.' Angela sat back in her chair with a huge sigh of relief.

'How does your husband feel about this?'

'He understands. It is just a matter of bringing closure to a traumatic event.'

Ian shook his head gently from side to side. 'I still think this is more a matter for a private detective. Why do you want to involve me?'

'I read what you did for your client, John Field, a couple of years ago. You are obviously a man of integrity and I need someone I can trust,' Angela said, giving Ian a look that any man would find hard to resist.

'Even if I was willing to help you, the partnership would never allow it,' Ian said reluctantly. 'It's just not what we do and I can't just abandon my other clients.'

'I've thought about that,' Angela said with a growing confidence. She pulled a cheque book out of her handbag and tore off a previously completed cheque made payable to Ryders. It was for £32,000.

'I have worked on the basis that I pay you £200 per hour which I suspect is higher than your normal charge out rate. Eight hours a day for a four-week period comes to £32,000. Show this to your partners and say I want you to go to Berlin to look into restitution of property and trace some family contacts. Say you are looking into whether my family property still exists and making contact with some German lawyers who can act on my behalf via Ryders acting as my Agents. Say, given my history, I am still too fearful to travel to East Germany myself or reveal my location.'

Ian was pensive. She had it all worked out. 'It could work,' he replied. 'Do you actually want me to look into restitution of property?'

'It's something we can factor in but it's secondary. My parents had a nice house just outside Berlin. My mother had died of breast cancer before I escaped and my father remarried. We didn't really get on. He always wanted a boy. He's dead now but it would be nice to know what happened to our property.'

Angela had an expression of excited anticipation on her face as she awaited Ian's decision. He sank back into his chair.

'Let me think about it. We have a partners' meeting tomorrow afternoon. I'll mention it and get back to you. Where are you staying?'

'I'll be hard to pin down so I'll ring you. Would tomorrow at 4.00pm be convenient?'

'That should be fine.'

'Good,' Angela said as she stood up and slid the cheque across the table.

That evening Ian went back to his home in Studley Roger. He had bought a little cottage a couple of years ago behind Lawrence House. It was one of several built around a grass square which was communal. Being gregarious, this was no problem for Ian but Sophie hated it. She didn't like the fact that there was no private outside space or the fact that everyone had their assigned roles. One man cut the grass, another took charge of the flower beds and there were lots of petty regulations such as when and where you could hang out washing. However, it had got Ian onto the property ladder and it was in his favourite village giving easy access to Studley Park and Fountains Abbey.

But Ian was feeling unsettled, so he did what he always did at such times and went on a run even though it was a dark, damp Wednesday night in November.

On such a miserable evening, the hardest thing to do is

to set off, so Ian put a dark grey sweatshirt over his t-shirt and started walking slowly from his house to the long entrance drive to the deer park, doing various loosening exercises along the way.

As he approached the magnificent archway that sat between Ripon Cathedral and St Mary's Church, he realised that the purple sky would not provide enough light to run off-road safely, so once over the cattle grids he started jogging and then he broke into a sprint to the brow of the hill. Ian then turned around and trotted back down the hill to the archway. He repeated this three times in five minutes and then rested for two sucking the air back into his lungs as his pounding heartbeat started to slow. He then did two reps in three minutes and again rested for two. Then he did one faster sprint in one minute twenty seconds, running as fast as he could. He then repeated this process in reverse, this time climbing the pyramid by doing a single rep, then a double and finishing on a triple.

By the last rep Ian was feeling strong. The hill climbs had worked his thigh muscles and now the flat road seemed easy. He ran out of the village, along a footpath to Ripon and taking the back roads he headed towards the nearby village of Littlethorpe.

He was mulling things over. Did he really want to go on another wild goose chase? It would be quite exciting and the money would massively help his annual billing target. He was usually only able to charge the equivalent of five hours a day as most property work was done on a fixed fee basis and he was under pressure to increase his billing especially since Mark Thompson, the new litigation partner, had been appointed. He was being encouraged to become more specialised and concentrate on Agricultural Law but still, this was no silver bullet.

The wind had picked up and cleared the sky of clouds revealing a beautiful star-lit canopy. Ian ran standing tall with his shoulders back taking in the galaxy. Sometimes the planets align. Some would call it coincidence; others would call it fate. Either way, as though drawn together by some invisible gravitational force, Ian was about to become an important link in a dramatic chain of events.

Suddenly, as he approached a smallholding, he stopped in his tracks. A farmer was corralling some geese into a wooden shed and a sheep dog, chained beside its kennel was jumping up and down, barking with excitement. The geese scattered and the farmer went up to the dog cursing and swiping at it with a piece of blue plastic piping. He was waving it wildly, the dog darting out of the way but a couple of blows hit the dog on its shoulders and then a crushing blow came down on the top of its head. The dog collapsed and appeared almost unconscious. Ian felt sick and an intense anger boiled inside him which he had to use all his self-discipline to restrain.

'Hey, stop,' Ian said, running over to the dog. He knelt down and looked at it lying on its side. There was no blood but the dog didn't react other than one slight lift of the tail as Ian ran his hand over the side of its head.

'Who the hell are you?' asked the farmer in a deep, gruff voice.

'I'm Ian Sutherland - a local solicitor. There is no way you should treat a dog like that.'

'I'll treat it however I fucking well want to treat it. It's my dog.' The man had a strange tone to his voice but Ian thought it might just be his age. Ian wanted to hit him but his mind was racing for a less drastic solution.

'I'll buy it from you,' Ian said impulsively and then after a slight pause, 'either that or I will report you to the RSPCA.'

The farmer straightened himself up and looked at Ian more intently. He was in his early seventies, unshaven with wild, mousey hair and a slightly stooped stature. He was wearing dirty, fawn-coloured trousers and braces over a checked woollen-mix shirt. He was thin and unkempt.

'If you're a solicitor you can make me a Will,' he said after some thought. 'You can have the dog if you make me a Will. She's no good to me.'

'Okay,' Ian replied without thinking it through. 'How about I call on you tomorrow morning on the way to work; about 9 o'clock?'

'That'll do,' the farmer said starting to relax his aggressive stance.

'But I'm taking the dog now,' Ian demanded. 'What's

she called?'

'Sky.'

Ian was still kneeling beside the dog and he undid the chain.

'Have you got a lead?'

The farmer pulled out some orange bailing twine from his pocket and tossed it at Ian. Ian tied one end to the collar and gave a little tug.

'Come on Sky.' The dog staggered to its feet and gingerly took a couple of paces towards Ian.

Ian looked back at the farmer. 'I'll see you tomorrow,' he said with the tone of a hard-nosed businessman concluding a deal.

They made it to the market square in Ripon but Sky was walking slowly and was unsteady on her feet so Ian went up to the taxi rank and persuaded one of the drivers to give them a lift home.

Ian made a bed for Sky out of an old duvet in the corner of the kitchen but she wouldn't eat or drink anything so Ian just sat on the floor stroking her. He couldn't believe he had landed himself with a dog but he should be able to find a better home for her and in the meantime his next-door neighbour, Nell, an elderly spinster, would be happy to look after her whilst he was at work.

The next morning Ian arranged an emergency appointment at the vets for 8.00am. John Foster, a jolly fellow, called them in.

'Sky Sutherland please.' Ian thought it funny that the vet had attached his surname to the name of the dog. It gave a sense of belonging.

Ian explained what had happened. 'I'm not even sure what sort of dog she is. She's got a long nose for a collie.'

Sky was tri-coloured. Black, white and tan with a hound like head and very pretty markings. Her body and the top of her head were mainly black but her neck, shoulders and front legs were white and she had a tan muzzle and eyebrows, and her back legs were tan coloured with white paws.

'That's because she's not a Border Collie but a Smooth Collie,' John said. 'Like Lassie but with a smooth coat.'

John examined her eyes and teeth; then he checked her pulse and temperature. He felt her all over and she whimpered when he ran his hands over her ribs. Finally, he lifted each leg individually and tested their movement.

'She's a bit dull. She may be concussed but otherwise she's okay. Nothing's broken. Take her home for a couple of days and see how she goes. If she doesn't pick up soon, bring her straight back.'

'Okay, thank you very much,' Ian replied as he headed for reception to pay the bill.

Ian took her home and left his house keys with Nell who said she would keep an eye on her, which probably meant she would sit with her all day. Then Ian had a quick shower, put on his suit and headed for Littlethorpe.

The smallholding looked different in the daylight. An ordinary red brick farmhouse sat in the centre of a two-acre site of over grazed grassland. Dozens of hens, ducks and geese roamed freely and shabby looking wooden sheds littered the land, spaced sporadically over the entire site.

Ian pulled his E-type Jaguar slowly off the main road, worried that the dirt track drive might be a host for rusty nails and foreign objects. He could see the back door was slightly ajar and a light was on so he made his way around the side of the house and tapped gently on the glass.

'Come in,' a voice shouted from within.

Ian pushed open the door and walked into the kitchen where the farmer was sat in an old threadbare armchair beside a glowing coal fire with a mug of hot tea.

Suddenly, the smell hit him and Ian physically pulled back. Such was the stench; it was like walking into a brick wall. A hen was pecking at the kitchen floor and the carcass of a new born kitten was burning on top of the coals. Ian hoped it had died of natural causes.

'Have a seat,' the farmer said pointing to a similar armchair opposite his own. Ian was worried about his Savile Row suit getting dirty so he positioned himself on the edge of the seat.

'I've just realised I don't even know your name,' Ian said thinking of the information he needed to do the Will so he could get out as quickly as possible.

'Tempest Huber,' the farmer replied.

'Tempest? That's unusual.'

'I was born during a storm so my mother called me Tempest.'

'Right, but I will have to use your real name for the Will although I can put, "also known as Tempest Huber," if you have used it in any official capacity.'

Tempest laughed but Ian wasn't sure why. 'It is my real name,' he replied.

'Okay, so what you would like to do?'

'Leave everything to my niece and nephew.'

'You're not married then?'

'No.'

'And you've no children?'

'No. There was just me and my sister and she died a few years ago, so now I just have my niece and nephew.'

'And you want to leave everything to them?'

'Yes.'

'Do they have any children?'

'No,' Tempest snapped getting a bit tired by the quick-fire questions. Ian picked up on this.

'Sorry about all the questions. We're nearly there. Do you want them as your executors?'

'What's that?'

'Well, the executors sort out your estate when you are gone and then distribute it to your beneficiaries.'

'Well, they can do that,' Tempest replied, as though it was obvious.

'Okay and what does your estate consist of?'

'What do you mean?'

'Well, I take it that you own this smallholding. What other property do you have?'

'Just a bit of money in the Building Society and the furniture,' Tempest said, waving his left arm towards some rooms beyond the kitchen. Ian didn't think it was worth taking a look.

'Okay, well I will get this drawn up for you as soon as possible.' Ian paused whilst he tried to decide whether to invite him to the office to sign his Will or risk another visit to the farmhouse. Neither alternative was attractive. 'Are you able to come to the office to sign the Will?'

'Are you in Ripon?'

'No, Harrogate.'

'Oh, I don't go that far! You'll have to come here,' Tempest replied in a way that made it clear Ian had no choice in the matter.

'Okay, I will get this typed up and come back as soon as I can. I will have to bring someone with me, though, because we need two witnesses. Have you got a phone number so I can let you know when it is ready?'

'Yes,' Tempest replied and he then enunciated the number.

Ian thought for a moment. It was important to get Wills signed as soon as possible and this one was quite straight forward.

'I tell you what. How about I come tomorrow, about 5 o'clock? That will save me trying to catch you in.'

'That'll do,' Tempest concluded.

Ian made a hasty exit and arrived at work just after 10.00am. He bypassed reception and bolted up the stairs to his office. Originally, the offices had been a Georgian townhouse and Mark Thompson was pacing up and down the landing, as was his habit, speaking into his Dictaphone. He usually did this at set times of the day, like first thing in the morning or going home time, to let others see he was still working whilst making the point that they were not.

'Good of you to come in,' he said sarcastically.

Ian had been made a partner a couple of years ago following his fame with the Field case but Mark Thompson had been brought in shortly afterwards and he was, what was known in the trade, as a "big gorilla." Six years older than Ian, he had a barrel shaped belly and an acid tongue. He brought in more money than any other partner and got recompensed accordingly. However, he was the only partner, other than fellow Geordie, Steven Fell, who had not been privately educated and he resented this. Most of all he resented Ian who was better looking, drove an E-type Jag, wore a Rolex and was clubbable in a way which he never would be. He was divisive with everyone and he knew how to push Ian's buttons.

'I've been with a client,' Ian replied defensively.

'It's not in your diary.'

'I only made the appointment last night. It's someone I met when I got home.'

'Save it for the partners' meeting,' Thompson said as he walked away disinterestedly.

Ian didn't reply but went and plonked himself down at his desk and let out a huge sigh. He was one of seven partners but he just couldn't compete with the fees brought in by the litigators who were able to charge by the hour. Angela's offer was starting to look more attractive although he felt this would only help him win a battle whilst losing the war. He let his mind drift back to Sky, sat at home in his kitchen.

'Well, at least someone appreciates me,' Ian mumbled to himself as he reached for a file. 'I may even have saved her life.' Little did he know it would be the other way around.

Chapter Three

Partners' meetings were not much fun and Ian was worried about the long-term prospects for the business.

The building was owned by a trust, the beneficiaries of which were members of the Ryder and Roberts families so the partnership paid rent for its use of the offices. That excluded the non-family partners from any benefit derived from increasing property prices and meant that the only assets of the business were unpaid bills, work-in-progress and a small amount for furniture and fittings. Offset against these was an overdraft.

Retiring partners had traditionally been bought out receiving full value for their capital accounts even though some bills never got paid and some work-in-progress was eventually written off.

The business was profitable but virtually all the income was withdrawn as partners' drawings which had been set at levels reflecting former glories rather than present day realities.

So, as a businessman, Ian saw a weak balance sheet, a changing marketplace and a lack of decisive management.

There were seven partners and, therefore, seven people

trying to manage the business to suit their own priorities.

Hannah Ryder was sixty and felt the responsibility of a third-generation steward. She had no vision of her own so listened intently to siren voices hoping that someone else would reveal a way forward.

Julie Short was fifty-five but married to a wealthy and much older man. Her eyes were fixed on early retirement but she liked being queen bee of the probate department which was profitable and added substantial sums to the client account. She was spoilt but she was a competent lawyer and as head of the most profitable department she had power. She was assisted by Michael Evans, ten years her junior; a very quiet and boring individual who was anxiously awaiting his turn to take her place although the second fiddle rarely played such a charismatic role.

Ronnie Roberts was fifty-one and had specialised in representing petty criminals in the Magistrates Court, conducting neighbourhood litigation and doing a bit of conveyancing and probate when he could be bothered to put his head down. With the tightening restrictions on Legal Aid, however, criminal law was proving unprofitable and he was struggling to find a useful role.

That left the three more recently appointed partners: Ian who had joined the firm to do Wills, Trusts, Probate and Property and Steven Fell, a litigator of the same age, who saw his route to success through being a collaborator with Mark Thompson; who six years their senior, arrived with a ready-made reputation as a rottweiler with the ability to increase fee income and provide fresh direction.

The partners met at 1.00pm in the board room. Situated on the first floor, with large sash windows providing views of Harrogate's parkland, known as "The Stray," they sat around an oblong mahogany table with a longcase clock in the corner and oil paintings on the walls. Supermarket sandwiches were served by Sarah with tea and coffee and an agenda was distributed by Mark Thompson, as approved by Hannah.

Hannah presented the financials and then the partners mooted important topics such as whether or not to adopt window envelopes and the length of the Christmas break. She then handed over to Mark Thompson who was meant to present a paper on the future direction of the firm.

He sat there looking cross. The large bulk of his torso bulging over the table contrasting with his thin arms and small hands. Square spectacles sat on his fat face which had the colour of someone with high blood pressure. It was a body that took no exercise but was fuelled for physical activity.

'Right,' he said, barely giving Hannah a chance to finish. 'My proposal is that we join the Personal Injury Group. Based in Newcastle they guarantee to send us four to five new cases a week for which we pay £250 each and 10% of any damages collected on behalf of the client.'

Ian did a quick calculation based on a forty-six-week

working year. 'That's around £50,000 per annum in referral fees before we've collected a penny, win or lose.'

Thompson nodded as though Ian was stating the obvious.

'That's peanuts compared with what I will bill. I expect to bring in £250,000 this year. What will you bill?' he paused to look at the management accounts. 'Oh, only half that,' he said feigning surprise.

Hannah gave a quick glare. She didn't like the fact that this was getting personal, especially so early on in the proceedings.

'I don't like the idea of paying for work and I've heard the files arrive in a white van,' Ronnie said with incredulity.

'Plus, it's not just about headline figures,' Ian persisted. 'Non-contentious work adds to our client account balance but these contingency fee cases will need financing from office account. The referral fees will need financing, the disbursements will need financing and the overheads will need financing, for a much longer period before we get paid.'

There was a gentle rumble of agreement around the table but Thompson hit straight back.

'You will all have to work harder or earn less. You're living in the past. School fees and holidays can't be paid for out of probate and conveyancing fees any longer.'

Ronnie looked worried. These items were high on his agenda.

'We've never done anything like this before,' Julie said.

'That's not an argument not to do it now,' Thompson retorted.

'Is there a danger we lose control over who we act for?' Gosh, Evans has said something, Ian thought, and it's not a bad question.

'Don't worry. I will deal with the shit as usual. You can all keep your Harrogate gentry.'

'That's enough,' Hannah interjected. 'This would be a major new venture for us and we are entitled to debate it with civility.' Thompson's face reddened. He didn't want to debate anything. By nature, he was a dictator and a bully.

Ian launched back in. 'My fear is we are trying to marry two completely different businesses. Both may have their merits but they have different business models and, brought together, they may cause a clash of cultures.'

Thompson stood up to leave. 'I'm offering to make you all rich but you are so short sighted you can't see it. We can bill half a million a year from this with Steve helping me and that's just the start. We have to develop a new source of income but you lot are completely blind to the dangers that lie ahead.'

Hannah started to panic. She had brought Thompson in to shake things up but she hadn't considered how he would do it and she was feeling very uncomfortable.

'Sit down and calm down. What I suggest is we try it for a year and see how we get on. We can always drop it if we don't like it.'

Murmurs of reluctant approval ran around the table although nothing emanated from Ian other than a sick feeling in the base of his stomach. He knew, one way or another, this would go wrong.

'Good, that's agreed then. Now, any other business?'

'Yes,' Ian started. 'I've had an unusual approach from a lady called Angela Jaeger. Originally from East Germany, she escaped to the West in 1963. She has said she would like me to go to Berlin to look into restitution of property, employ some German lawyers as our Agents and look up a couple of relatives.'

'Why am I not surprised?' Thompson asked sarcastically.

'It seems highly unusual to me,' Ronnie said. 'Why should we get involved and what about your workload?'

'Well, I can manage that and Ed can help,' Ian replied, referring to Ed Tucker a trainee solicitor with Ryders who Ian had taken under his wing. 'He's doing a really good job.'

'It sounds like another John Field case to me and whilst you are obviously adept at dealing with such situations, I am not sure it is something we should encourage.' Hannah's initial response was not what Ian wanted. He needed her on side or there was no chance of getting it past the others. He slid the cheque across the table.

'She gave me this. It represents four weeks' work at

£200 per hour for eight hours a day.'

Thompson reached for the cheque and swivelled it around. There was a pause and you could almost see the cogs turning.

'No, I think he should go. We can manage things here.' There was a slight menace in his voice. *Easily manage* was the implication.

Not surprisingly, the money clinched it. Ian's request was agreed and with business concluded for the time being they all filed out of the board room and headed for their individual offices. Mark Thompson sank into his large leather armchair and called his secretary from the adjacent room. She wasn't actually his secretary because Ryders worked in teams but Tracy Davy and Cheryl Jones worked for Thompson and Fell which was a higher ratio of support than the other partners but Thompson had insisted it was necessary.

'You look tired,' Tracy said as she walked in, went behind his desk and stood beside him. 'Would you like me to make you a drink?' She asked putting her hand on his shoulder.

Tracy had curly brown hair and bright red lipstick. She was wearing a silky dark red blouse, a short black skirt and knee-high black, high-heeled boots.

Thompson let his hand slip from the side of his chair to the side of her boot and he caressed it gently.

'Tea please. Oh, and I'm giving you a rise. I got the

Personal Injury Group past that twat Sutherland so you and Cheryl are going to have a lot more work to do now. I will tell accounts you are both going up to £20,000 per annum with immediate effect.'

Tracy lent forward and planted a kiss on the side of his cheek leaving a mark with her lipstick.

'I thought I was giving you one,' she teased.

'One what?'

'A rise!'

'Out!' Thompson said affectionately, slapping her backside as she turned to leave.

Ian had obtained the approval he needed but he wasn't happy. The atmosphere was becoming stifling and he was looking forward to getting out of the office. Just Sophie to get it past now but she wasn't back until tomorrow.

Suddenly, his phone rang and brought him back to reality with a start.

'Angela Jaeger for you,' said the receptionist.

'Gosh is it that time already?' Ian asked looking at his watch. 'Thank you, Sarah. Put her through.'

'How was your partners' meeting?' Angela asked.

'Fine, I've got the green light to go. I will need expenses, though, as the cheque you've given me is for my time. I suggest I use some of that for expenses and then you can make up the difference?'

'That's fine, Ian. I am just relieved you have the agreement we needed. When can you go?'

'I'm hoping to go next week. What information can you give me?'

'Just his mother's address I'm afraid and that was from twenty-six years ago but hopefully she will still be there. She will be in her early seventies by now but it was a rented apartment owned by the government so she is unlikely to have moved.'

'If she's still alive,' Ian muttered to himself.

'Pardon?'

'I said, I hope she's still alive.'

'Quite so. Oh, and one other thing. They know me as Angelika. I've only used Angela since I left Germany. Good luck.'

'Thanks,' Ian said somewhat disheartened. 'I'll keep in touch.'

Ian pushed the Jag through its paces to get home to Sky, gripping the wooden steering wheel as he navigated the corners. He loved the little circular dials on the dashboard, feeding back information as to how the car was feeling. 'We're all good,' he said, by way of reassurance to himself.

Nell was waiting for him in the kitchen. She was a large, manly looking woman in her late sixties. Unmarried, she had spent her working life as a bus driver but now she only rode a bicycle, with a basket at the front for her shopping. She didn't really like people, but she loved animals so she was friendly with Ian because she knew he was fond of animals too.

'She hasn't eaten anything all day and she's very subdued,' Nell said, almost confrontationally. She had no time for small talk.

'Well thank you for looking after her, Nell. I'll try her with something from the fridge.'

'Humph!' she snorted in disbelief that Ian could succeed where she had failed. 'I'd like to get my hands on the bugger that hit her; that's all,' Nell remonstrated as she turned to go home, muttering to herself as she walked away.

Ian pulled out a packet of salami and offered one of the circular slices to Sky in the hope that the strong smell would arouse her appetite but she looked at it and turned away. Ian was worried. She hadn't eaten anything since he brought her home last night. He sat down on the duvet next to her and stroked her gently. Taking a piece of salami, he placed it between her paws and, after she had sniffed it, he started to slowly pull it away. Sky stopped it with her paw and ate it quickly. Ian then repeated this successfully eight times after which Sky refused the ninth piece but stood up and had a drink of water.

They had turned a corner. Ian knew she would be all right now and he was looking forward to introducing her to Sophie tomorrow.

'I wonder if we could keep you?' he asked her, teasingly. 'You won't fit in the E-type but Sophie's Mercedes has a back seat. I could take you for a walk before work and then Nell could keep an eye on you during the day. Plus, with Sophie working at Durham University she gets long holidays.'

Sky didn't need much convincing. She had rested her head on Ian's thigh so he couldn't move without disturbing her which he didn't want to do. Instead, he just sat with her relaxing and contemplating the day. There was some merit in Mark Thompson's arguments but the Personal Injury Group was not the solution. He visualised the capital letters from the Agenda.

'It's a PIG Sky. It's an absolute PIG.'

The next morning Ian briefed Ed Tucker about Tempest Huber and they agreed to leave work about 4.15pm and travel in two separate cars to the smallholding on the outskirts of Ripon so Ed could make his own way home straight afterwards. Ian did not feel it was the sort of place to take one of the secretaries and it would be a good experience for Ed.

Time hadn't mellowed the impact of the vision Tempest's home presented. It looked like a shanty town from a TV news report on overcrowding and poverty in a Third World country. Hen huts were everywhere, wooden pallets and chicken wire made up temporary enclosures and poultry of all sorts wandered about freely.

Tempest was in the kitchen which appeared to be the only room in the house in regular use. The smell was horrific. A cat sat on the dresser but it wasn't the source of the problem. It was just general filth and chicken droppings inside the house. In fact, there was little differentiation between the inside and outside; one just merged into the other.

Ed was looking gravely pale and Ian was worried that he would either faint or throw up. Consequently, this was a Will which was going to receive the minimum of explanations.

'I've got your Will for you Mr Huber,' Ian said handing it over. 'It's very straightforward. It appoints your niece and nephew as Executors and leaves everything to them in equal shares. Should one of them predecease you the other will inherit everything as neither of them has any children.'

'Very good,' Tempest said nodding to indicate he understood.

'Have you any questions?'

'No, I can't say I do.'

'Right, well if you would just like to sign here.' Ian pointed to the appropriate place and handed over one of the cheap, branded, Ryders biros. Tempest scrawled his signature and passed back the biro.

'You can keep that,' Ian said signing underneath with his own pen and then passing the Will to Ed who also signed the Will and then dated it.

Job done they made a hasty retreat to the cars. Ian was looking forward to being home at a reasonable time for Sophie but Ed stopped him as he went to open the car door.

'Can I have a quick word with you please?' Ed looked deadly worried.

'Yes, what's up?'

'You know meeting rooms five and six were originally one room which has been divided by a thin partition wall?'

'Yes.'

'Well, I was using room six as a quiet room this morning to do some research and Mark Thompson and Steven Fell went into room five for a meeting and I heard every word they said.'

'And?'

'They rang Counsel and put him on speaker phone. They asked how they could get rid of you if there was no partnership agreement. Counsel said any partner could dissolve the partnership and then there would be a division of assets which Mark Thompson said was not a problem because Ryders hardly had any assets and he could easily run up the overdraft. He then told Steve to go through all your files when you go to Germany to see if they can find anything to use against you.'

Ian put his arm on Ed's shoulder. Ed was still pale and Ian was disappointed although not surprised by what he was hearing.

'I'm really grateful you told me this but don't worry about it,' Ian said reassuringly. 'If I can outwit the Nazis a couple of backstabbing litigators shouldn't be a problem.'

Chapter Four

Ian arrived home before Sophie got back from Durham so he opened a bottle of Chianti Riserva and started the preparations for a Spaghetti Bolognese whilst he awaited her return. Sophie had moved from Munich and secured a lectureship at Durham University in the history department. They felt it was too far for a daily commute so she based herself in one of the colleges and stayed with Ian at weekends. It was a sort of half-way house to setting up home together but she wasn't too happy about the half-way bit and as the cottage belonged to Ian, she hadn't managed to put her stamp on it.

'Who's this?' Sophie asked as she opened the door and Sky trotted up to see her.

'Her name is Sky. She's decided to join the family.'

Sophie dropped her bags in the hall and came into the kitchen.

'Are you serious?' She asked looking hopefully into Ian's eyes.

'Well, I rescued her from a farmer who was mistreating her and didn't think much past getting her out of his way. I thought I could re-home her but I like having her around and Nell says she will help look after her. So, if it's okay with you, I thought we could keep her?'

Sophie threw her arms around his neck and kissed him. 'Of course, it's okay with me.'

Ian carried on chopping the onions and said that was why his eyes were watering. 'I saw him hit her on the head with a plastic pipe so I took her to the vets and they thought she might be concussed but she seems all right now. She wouldn't eat anything to start with though.'

'Oh, you poor thing,' Sophie said kneeling down to stroke her. 'You will have to have some Spaghetti Bolognese to help build you up again.' Sky wagged her tail in agreement.

So far so good. Ian knew the first topic of conversation would be an easy win. He just had to tell her about Angela now.

'I'm afraid I've got to go to Berlin next week. I've got a new client called Angela and she wants me to go and find an ex-boyfriend who got stuck behind the Berlin Wall when they attempted an escape together in 1963, and she also wants me to look into restitution of her family property.'

Ian handed Sophie a glass of wine.

'But I can't go next week. It's the middle of term.'

'I know. I just thought I would make a flying visit. I'll only be gone two or three days.'

'What about Sky?'

'I thought Nell could look after her.'

'That's not fair at her age. It's one thing to let a dog out at lunchtime but you can't expect Nell to take her for walks. Anyway, Sky will get confused. She will have to come back to Durham with me.'

'Are you allowed dogs in college?'

'Yes,' Sophie replied in a way which made it absolutely clear it was not a matter for negotiation.

Early the following week Ian arrived at Kings Cross and took a taxi straight to Chancery Lane and the offices of Falcon Storrs-Fox, a niche firm of solicitors specialising in partnership disputes and other esoteric areas of the law.

Ian had made an appointment to see Sean Blake, an old colleague from his days as an articled clerk in Leeds. Sean had a razor-sharp mind and a clarity of thinking which was amazing to observe. You could present him with a situation of garbled facts and he would respond with a crystal-clear analysis and bullet point plan to take things forward, and if you said anything illogical, he was on to it immediately.

The offices were built in the classical style with arched windows and pediments and pink painted plastering on the frontage but the building was tall and narrow with small square rooms overcrowded with solicitors and support staff so Sean greeted Ian in reception and suggested they withdrew for lunch at Simpson's, the famous restaurant in The Strand.

They walked past the Royal Courts of Justice, on their

right, and Ian marvelled at the sheer size and stature of the building. It signified power and strength but it was the power of the Rule of Law. The independent judiciary could hold the Government to account. They were an essential pillar of democracy and Ian felt a rush of pride that he was a solicitor and part of the justice system. They continued past Somerset House, on their left, swapping small talk and legal gossip until Ian stopped suddenly and stood back as they reached their destination. The entrance was magnificent. A pale grey stone archway guarded by black wrought iron gates stood in front of them, with copper panels affixed to each gate saying "Simpson's". Either side of the archway were stone pillars with brass shields saying "Simpson's Divan Tavern" and above the archway, the name was marked again in gold lettering, each letter being over one foot high. Around the top of the archway were large red and white tiles, designed to look like a chess board and on some of the tiles gold coloured chess pieces were incised.

'That's unusual,' Ian commented, pointing up to the top of the entrance. 'It looks like a chess board.'

Sean laughed. 'That's because Simpson's started out as a chess club in 1828. I thought it a rather fitting place to meet, given that we need to come up with a strategy to deal with your office politics.'

'Gosh, I had no idea,' Ian replied, as he gazed around still taking in his surroundings.

Ian also realised that Sean was meeting him in his lunch hour and, as a professional courtesy, would not be logging any time so Ian was relieved that, at least, he could buy Sean a decent lunch.

They sat down at a small round table with a white table cloth, silver cutlery and comfortably curved red leather chairs.

The food was traditional English fare designed to keep the upper classes firmly within their comfort zone so they both ordered Beef Wellington and a glass of red wine.

'So, give me the details,' Sean said once they had completed all the pleasantries.

'I'm just not happy at Ryders,' Ian replied. 'There are two problems. Firstly, I think the new litigation partner wants rid of me. Well, no, actually - I know he does. One of the trainee solicitors overheard him saying as much to Counsel; and secondly, I think the firm lacks leadership and direction, but I am not in a position to turn things around. There are too many partners each paddling their own canoes.'

'That's not uncommon in a partnership. Does Ryders have a written partnership agreement?'

'No, we could never agree on one so we just rely on the Partnership Act 1890,' Ian admitted with some embarrassment.

'As do most firms,' Sean replied reassuringly. 'In fact, I rarely see a firm of solicitors with a partnership agreement unless it's one of the majors. That's not a problem, though. The 1890 Act is well drafted and straightforward so it should work in your favour. It's fair, whereas a partnership agreement would probably give a majority of partners an unfair advantage.'

'How do you mean?' Ian asked, his hopes rising.

'Well for a start, you have the benefit of section 25. No majority of partners can expel another so they can't get rid of you unless they dissolve the partnership and that has potential tax disadvantages. You can just sit there and take your share of the profits until they negotiate a fair settlement.'

'I'm not sure I follow.' Ian furrowed his forehead and Sean continued.

'Partnership agreements often contain things that certain partners don't like, such as the imposition of restrictive covenants on a departing partner, so more often than not the partners can't come to a consensus and they end up relying on the Partnership Act 1890 which is almost a hundred years old. Consequently, because the Act doesn't provide for the expulsion of a partner, the only way to get rid of someone is by dissolving the partnership. Not only can this have adverse tax consequences but it also triggers a valuation of partnership assets and the surplus assets, after payment of debts and liabilities, are then payable to the partners in accordance with their share of the capital and profits.'

Ian's hopes deflated. 'Ryders hasn't got many assets I'm afraid. Just work-in-progress and unpaid bills plus a small amount for office fittings, and they are offset by an overdraft.'

'What about goodwill?'

'It's never been valued. Incoming partners don't pay for it upon entering the partnership and outgoing partners don't get paid for it on retirement.'

'That doesn't mean it doesn't exist,' Sean retorted. 'Anyway, what you describe is what has traditionally happened in cases of retirement where the partners have signed an election to continue the partnership. On a dissolution it's all up for grabs.'

Ian wanted to believe Sean but was worried this was too good to be true. 'I'm not sure how you would value goodwill. How do you know what it's worth?'

'You apply to the Court to wind up the business. There are more assets than you think. There is value in the name Ryders because it is well known and trusted. There is value in the phone number because that is the first point of contact when a client wants to get in touch and there is value in the location of the premises – in other words the lease. All these things make up the goodwill and it is worth whatever anyone is willing to pay for it.'

The penny started to drop and Ian sat there in silence as he mulled over Sean's words and knocked back the last of his wine. Eventually, he beamed with excitement.

'You've given me an idea; a really good idea. Thanks Sean; I'll work on it.'

'Leave the accounts with me and I will have a look through them and, in the meantime, just shout if you need any more help.'

A waitress came to clear away their plates and after coffee they said their good-byes and Ian made a dash for Bond Street.

Ian was disappointed not to be visiting his friends at Anderson & Sheppard the tailors and he felt a pang of regret not to be staying at The Ritz again but he did have one little treat up his sleeve.

He darted into the Royal Arcade and rang the bell to the premises of George Cleverley the shoemakers. Ever since he had broken his ankle, he had struggled to get shoes to fit, as his right foot seemed to have widened, so he was joining the ranks of the elite who had their shoes made to measure.

A young gentleman opened the door.

'Hello, I've come to collect some shoes please,' Ian said as he entered the small room with its large curved glass window.

'And your name, Sir?'

'Ian Sutherland.'

'Very good, Sir. I will just get the shoemaker for you.'

There were two reasons why people bought bespoke shoes. One was for the fit and the other for the material.

Cleverley's clientele included pop stars and film stars from across the world who sometimes favoured the exotic. If you wanted your shoes made out of lizard and coloured green, they could do it. Ian's taste was far more conservative but as he was having them made, he thought he might as well have something a little more special so he had chosen Russian leather. This had been salvaged from a shipwreck off the Plymouth Sound and after almost two hundred years under water, the leather had acquired special qualities.

Preserved by airless black mud at the bottom of Plymouth Sound, this Russian leather which had been tanned in pits with willow bark and birch oil, was renowned for its ability to resist water.

John, the shoemaker, came down the spiral staircase and presented Ian with his shoes. The cross hatched grain, embossed by hand, gave the leather both texture and a differentiation in colour. Shades of tan, chestnut and a darker brown caught the light in varying degrees, highlighting the handiwork of the tanners.

Ian slipped on the shoes and knew instantly the fit was good.

'More like gloves!' he said.

Reluctantly, Ian took off the shoes, popped them into his suitcase and putting his black shoes back on, he headed for Heathrow.

It might sound glamorous to say, "I had lunch in London and dinner in Berlin," but Ian was on expenses, so he had booked a clean but cheap hotel in the Mitte district of the city which was close to the address he had for Theo's mother; and, as he didn't like eating alone, he had just consumed a beer and some currywurst on the street and then gone to bed wishing he had stuck to his usual, more healthy diet.

The next morning Ian walked to the address given to him by Angela. At first, he thought he was approaching a row of houses but then Ian realised they were actually apartments. The buildings appeared to be three storeys high and looked to have six apartments in each block. Every block was identical with an off-white, rendered frontage and a grey tiled roof. They were built in quadrangles around a small communal garden. Ian found a panel on the wall with doorbells and names beside them and to his surprise one said: "R. Hoffmann." He rang the bell and held his breath. He realised that Sophie's interpretation skills would have been useful but he would just have to manage without her. A lady in her mid-seventies came to the door.

'Hello, I'm looking for Theo,' Ian said a little hesitantly.

The lady looked at him with suspicion. She was slim with a well-lined face and dyed, fox-coloured hair. She looked as though she had endured a lifetime of hard work and Ian thought her trim stature was probably a consequence of lack of funds rather than a choice of lifestyle.

'I have come on behalf of Angelika Jaeger with some information for him,' Ian said quickly trying to explain his presence on her doorstep.

'What does she want after all this time?' She asked, spitting the words out with disgust.

'Now that the Wall has come down, she wants to make contact with him and, perhaps, help him financially.' An offer of money usually grabs people's attention, Ian thought.

The lady eyed him up closely. He was an unlikely stooge for the Stasi and so she felt she could probably take his words at face value.

'He won't be interested in her money; he's a Lutheran pastor now and I don't think he should speak to her,' she paused, 'but it's his decision. You can find him at St Mary's Church. Just head for Alexanderplatz and you will see it.' She closed the door just as Ian said: 'thank you.'

She was spot on with her directions. The pale brick church was set at an angle on Karl-Liebknecht Strasse on a square of landscaped concrete. The dusty pink walls were topped by a bright red tile roof, a sand-coloured brick tower and a blued, copper steeple. Other than the colour of the building materials, however, architecturally it looked like any other 19th century church in England, although its origins were much earlier.

There was a prominent statue of Martin Luther outside the church and Ian paused to look at it. Ian didn't know much about this seminal figure of the Reformation other than he had fallen out with the Roman Catholic Church especially over their practice of indulgences. Logically, this seemed right to Ian. Salvation by faith alone put God first. Indulgences gave the Church power and control.

Ian entered the church through some large oak doors and an elderly lady greeted him.

'Welcome to St Mary's,' she said.

'Thank you. I'm looking for Pastor Hoffman.'

The lady pointed down the aisle to where a small group of people stood singing to the left of the Altar.

They were practicing *Silent Night* in preparation for the Christmas celebrations so Ian sat at a pew, in the front row and listened until they had finished. There was one man amongst them, wearing a clerical collar and dark grey suit so, as the group broke up, Ian approached him.

'Excuse me. Are you Pastor Theo Hoffman by any chance?'

The man turned towards Ian. He had dark, wire like, ginger hair and was of medium build and height. He, perhaps, carried a little too much weight but Berlin was packed with excellent cafés and it looked as though this man enjoyed his cakes.

'Yes, that's me,' he said with an air of enquiry.

'My name is Ian Sutherland. I am a lawyer from England and I am here on behalf of Angelika Jaeger. She asked me to come here and find you.'

Theo looked stunned and stood there in silence. After a while he said: 'please come this way.'

He led Ian to a pew about half way down the aisle and they sat in the middle of a row as far away from anyone else as possible.

'This has come as a bit of a shock to me,' Theo said gently. 'I haven't seen Angelika for twenty-six years. Did she tell you how we were separated?'

'Yes. She said you were trying to escape across the border and she got through but you got caught.'

'Yes, I got caught,' Theo sighed. 'How is she?'

'She's very well. She has a successful business in Ireland. She owns caravan sites near sailing centres.'

Theo nodded. 'There was never any doubt that she would be successful. Is she married?'

'Yes, but she didn't marry until she was forty,' Ian said, trying to be sensitive because he could see the answers were important to Theo.

'Children?'

'A daughter aged nine.'

Theo was nodding. 'Do you know the name of her husband?'

'I think she said he was called Aidan O'Sullivan.'

Theo made a *huh* sound and suddenly went visibly pale. Ian noticed one of his eye sockets was indented and it started twitching.

'I have to go,' Theo said after a short silence, and he

stood up.

Ian could see the man needed some space; however, he couldn't leave things there.

'I do have some more things to discuss with you, if you can spare the time.'

Theo paused momentarily. 'Meet me at Café Kranzler this afternoon at, say, 3.30pm. It's just West of here near the Zoologischer Garten,' and with that, he left.

Five minutes before the appointed time, Ian stood outside the café feeling a little conspicuous and hoping that Theo would be punctual. He was, and Ian saw him well in advance as he walked across the square towards the café. He was wearing jeans, an open-necked, dark blue shirt and a suede jacket which Ian quite admired although it was the wrong colour for Theo. His skin pallor was too fair to provide the necessary contrast.

'Thank you for coming,' Ian said shaking Theo's hand. 'It is good of you to meet me.'

'Curiosity got the better of me. I just hope I don't turn out like the cat!'

They both laughed gently, went inside and sat at one of the tables. Both asked for cappuccinos and Theo ordered a slice of Schwarzwalder Kirschtorte. It looked good but Ian didn't like cherries so he ordered a Haselnuss Kunchen.

'So, what do you want to talk to me about?' Theo had regained his composure.

'Now that the Berlin Wall has fallen, Angelika wanted

me to make contact with you. I think she felt apprehensive before, being an escapee. She would like to see you again and, perhaps, help you financially, if you wanted to move from East Germany.'

Theo looked at Ian and gave him a kindly smile although the gaps in his teeth were a little disconcerting.

'God works in mysterious ways, Ian. If my attempted escape had been successful, it would have resulted in me leaving my mother behind. Angelika had no family ties but I did. I had a silly notion that I would send for my mother once I had gained my freedom but it would not have been possible – until now, perhaps.'

Ian was listening carefully but said nothing.

'Prison was hard but once released I was able to be a real help to my mother and my congregation, of course. I realised, it is people that matter and we are happiest when helping each other. I just wish God could have got his message across a little more gently!' Theo laughed again and took a sip of coffee. Ian noticed Theo's hand shake as he lifted the cup.

'No, my home is here, Ian, but thank Angelika for the offer.'

'What about meeting up with her? Is that something you would be willing to do?'

Theo swirled his plate around so that the narrow end of the cake was facing him and he helped himself to a fork full. He then washed it down with a gulp of coffee. It gave him time to think.

'There is something I would have to do first and it requires your help,' he said, almost whispering.

'My help?' Ian asked. Theo nodded.

'My father was Tyrolean. He was brilliant with figures and worked for the Vatican Bank. He met my mother just before the outbreak of War and I was the result! They married but he continued working for the Vatican, living in Rome, whilst my mother, grandmother and I stayed in Berlin. I think they just thought it was the safest and economically most viable option.

After the War this arrangement continued although I understand the eventual plan was to set up home together. The problem was my mother wanted it to be in Germany and my father wanted it to be in Italy. I think my mother would have won the argument, in the end, but straight after the War, Berlin was in turmoil and my father had a good job in Rome.'

Theo paused and looked into Ian's eyes.

'That all makes sense,' Ian said, seeing that a response was required.

'There were a lot of refugees after the War and the Vatican helped re-home them. They liaised with the International Red Cross to provide identity papers and used their contacts throughout the church worldwide to get visas for emigration. Many went to Argentina and other countries where the Catholic Church had strong relationships.'

Ian raised his eyebrows at the word *Argentina* and wondered where this was going.

'Many of these refugees changed their names. They wanted to leave their pasts behind them and make a fresh start. The church helped them financially and this, naturally, involved my father.'

'Okay,' Ian said slowly as the mystery unfolded.

'My father had concerns that some of these people were Nazis, escaping justice, but he was reassured that they were merely foot soldiers, following orders, so he went along with it, reluctantly. Then one day, in 1947, the paperwork for a prominent Nazi came in front of him. I don't know who it was or what he had done but it was a step too far for my father.'

Ian was listening intently. 'So, what did he do?' he asked.

'He wanted to become a whistle-blower but there was a problem.' Theo paused for dramatic effect. 'This Nazi was emigrating to Britain.'

'Hang on, hang on,' Ian said. 'You're going too fast for me. Firstly, why would the Catholic Church want to help a prominent Nazi escape after the War and secondly, why would he be allowed to emigrate to Britain?'

'That's what I want to find out.'

'I'm sorry,' Ian said, 'but I find this all a little hard to believe.'

Theo sat upright and took a different tack.

'Have you heard of Otto Eichmann?' he asked.

Ian shook his head.

'He was one of the chief architects of the Holocaust. In 1950 he fled to Argentina with the help of a bishop called Alois Hudal. He had been given a new identity under the name Ricardo Klement, so whatever it was that concerned my father in 1947, the church was still involved with in 1950.'

'How do you know all this?'

'It's public knowledge. In 1962 Eichmann's true identity was discovered so the Israelis carried out a covert operation, smuggled him out of Argentina and took him to Israel where he was tried and executed. It was all well publicised at the time.'

'I was only two,' Ian said, a little defensively.

'Of course, forgive me. I wasn't implying you should know these things. I was only offering it as evidence of what the Vatican was up to. My concern is that the 1947 Nazi is still at large and probably in Britain.'

'So, what happened to your father?'

'He was trying to work out who to inform. He didn't think he could go to the Western Intelligence Services because if this Nazi was moving to Britain, presumably, they already knew. However, before he could do anything he died of food poisoning.'

'Crikey. How did that happen?' Ian asked anxiously.

'I don't know and I'll probably never know, but before he died, he telephoned my mother and gave her the information I have just shared with you and he said he was sending her a watch, a deck watch. He said the watch contained the key to the whereabouts of the information which he had hidden regarding the Nazi moving to Britain. For some reason, he thought it of crucial importance. He was very anxious about it.'

'Did the watch arrive?'

'Yes, but after his death my mother wasn't really interested and she didn't want any trouble. I was only about seven at the time. When I was older, she told me the story and gave me the watch.'

'So where is it now?'

'That's where you come in. I gave it to Angelika.'

Ian sat back, put his hands behind his head and stared at the brightly lit ceiling.

'Does Angelika realise the significance of the watch?'

'No.'

'Didn't you try and work out the secret before you gave it to her?'

'Yes, I opened it up but there's nothing inside it. I didn't try very hard though. When I was young, I thought only of the future. Now the past seems more important.'

'What are you seeking to achieve? Revenge?'

'No. "Vengeance is mine, I will repay," says the Lord. I am looking for the truth. I want to expose the truth so the church is pressured into putting things right, or making recompense or, at least being prevented from letting it happen again.'

'So, you want me to go back to Angelika, get the watch and bring it back to you? Is that what you are asking?'

'Yes.'

'Then will you meet her?'

'After we have discovered its secrets, yes.'

'We?' Ian asked, recoiling at the suggestion.

'Something tells me you are here for a reason, Ian,' Theo said softly, looking into his eyes.

Ian finished the last swig of his coffee. It was a fascinating story and he felt a frisson of excitement at the prospect of being part of it. What he didn't know was that a similar story was just being told to someone else.

Chapter Five

Peter Schulz had waited almost his entire career to capture "the Shepherd" and now, when it was almost too late, as the German Democratic Republic descended into chaos before the reunification between East and West, his wish had been granted.

With the fall of the Berlin Wall, people's guards had come down, tongues had wagged and before he could really celebrate, Frank Schafer found himself bundled into the back of a black Mercedes E-class saloon and whisked off to the Stasi interrogation custody centre in the heart of the Forbidden Area.

He had been softened up in the usual way although now the methods were far less physical. The Stasi concentrated on psychological torture, trying to destroying the mind.

Schulz entered the room where Schafer was sat on a similar stool to that which Theo had perched on twenty-six years ago. His head was slumped on the table and he looked exhausted but, like Theo, his first sensory perception was the foul smell of stale tobacco and garlic.

'All this time I thought Schafer was a nickname,' Schulz laughed, mockingly. 'That you were shepherding your people to the West like some biblical hero; but now I discover it is simply your real name. You are not a hero in the eyes of the people but a mere profiteer. A capitalist feeding false hope to the misguided, not caring what happens to them once you have got their money. Do you know how many you helped to escape died in the process?'

Schafer lifted his head and stared at Schulz. The black greasy hair was now streaked with grey and he was a few pounds heavier, but the eyes were the same - mean and calculating.

'I know people were prepared to die to get away from the oppression of the Stasi and the communist regime.'

'Is that how you justify your hairbrained ideas? Hiding people in the back of vehicles, sending them down sewers, getting them to swim across the canals in the middle of the night? Don't you think we check these things?'

'Many of the attempts were successful,' Schafer countered.

'Good. That is an important admission which we can use against you in court.' Schulz smiled to let Schafer know he had just fallen into a trap.

'You won't be around long enough to take me to court. Your time is coming to an end,' Schafer said confidently.

'There is still time to do you some harm,' Schulz replied reassuringly. 'You don't know your history, Schafer. Look how many prisoners were killed in the last few weeks of the War. When a regime is coming to an end it wants to leaves things tidy.'

Schafer's head fell into his hands. He couldn't take much more of this; he was just so tired.

'I first heard about you from Theo Hoffmann.' Schafer looked up. Schulz had grabbed his attention. 'He was one of your failures. He ended up in prison you know?'

'I heard,' Schafer grunted in response.

'It affected him quite badly. He's a pastor now. Perhaps, he's looking for forgiveness after betraying you.'

'He wouldn't betray me,' Schafer said angrily.

'He told us all about you. Your name, how you stole the car, how much you charged for the passport and the visa, the places you operated from. We got it all from Hoffmann. But don't blame him. He was a broken man after we revealed his precious fiancée was deceiving him by screwing another man. I knew he would give up his secrets in the end.'

Schafer raised his head again and looked Schulz in the eye. He was angry to learn that Theo had betrayed him.

'He didn't.'

'He didn't what?' There was just the hint of anxiety in Schulz's voice.

'He didn't give up his secret.'

'What are you talking about?'

'Hoffmann has a much deeper secret and you didn't get it out of him.'

Schulz was perturbed. He didn't like the idea of

something getting past him. He considered himself a master of interrogation and the thought that Hoffmann had hoodwinked him was unsettling.

'Tell me then, what is this secret?'

Schafer laughed. 'Why should I?'

Schulz turned his back on Schafer, walker over to the window and stared out, over the barren, semi-derelict vista that comprised the Forbidden Area. Cracked concrete, broken fences, dilapidated buildings and barbed wire. Wherever he went, there was always barbed wire.

Schulz was a practical man. He did not let feelings get in his way. He looked at things objectively and Schafer was right. The regime was collapsing and in a short space of time the Stasi would be history. There would be investigations and recriminations. It was time for him to get out and what he needed now was information. Information that he could use for his future. He had waited years to capture Schafer but it was of no matter. Schafer now had a different purpose, that was all. None of this had ever been personal – he was just doing his job. He turned back and faced Schafer.

'If the information you have is useful, I will let you go,' he said impulsively.

'And you expect me to trust you?' Schafer replied almost breaking into a laugh again. He was the one mocking now.

'Come with me. I will personally drive you back to

the centre of town. Just you and me. You can tell me your story on the way and then get out. If you think we will come after you, I am sure you can find somewhere to hide.'

Schafer looked at Schulz carefully. He knew you should never trust the Stasi, but Schulz was convincing, and the alternative was bleak. He was desperate to get out of the Stasi's clutches and besides, he no longer felt any obligation to Theo. He thought they were friends but Theo had compromised his safety. There was no harm in revealing Theo's back story to get himself out of trouble, he reasoned.

'Okay,' he said thoughtfully.

Schafer was taken to his cell to change back into his civilian clothes and a guard brought him down to the entrance where Schulz was waiting beside the black Mercedes. He got in the front passenger seat and made sure that the door remained unlocked. Schulz started the engine and pulled away slowly.

'Now, tell me what this is all about and don't leave anything out.'

Schafer took a deep breath.

'Theo's father was a brilliant mathematician. He could add up several columns of figures at the same time and, as I was a childhood neighbour, he showed us some mathematical tricks when he was visiting. He was good with puzzles and that sort of thing. He worked for the Vatican Bank, though, and he lived in Rome so we only saw him occasionally.'

'What was his father's name?'

'Werner Hoffman.' Schafer paused.

'Carry on,' Schulz said.

'Anyway, one day, my mother said he had died from eating something poisonous. She took me to see Theo but he was distraught. He wouldn't say anything. He just sat in the corner of the kitchen holding a large pocket watch in his hands, which had been sent home by his father. He just kept turning it over and over. Years later he told me it contained the key to a secret. I asked him what the secret was and he said his father had details of a high-ranking Nazi refugee that the Vatican had smuggled out of Germany to Britain. The trouble was his father hadn't known who to trust as, apparently, British Intelligence knew all about it.'

'How can the watch contain the key to the secret?'

'I don't know. He thought that maybe the serial number was a combination to a safe deposit box or something like that but, if so, there was nothing to indicate where it was located.'

'And Theo Hoffman still has this watch?'

'No, he gave it to his fiancée just before they made their escape, so it is wherever she is, if she still has it.'

Schulz gave a wry smile which Schafer thought slightly strange.

'Is there anything else you can tell me?'

'I don't think so,' Schafer replied keen to make his exit.

Schulz stopped the car outside one of the S-Bahn terminals. 'Thank you, Herr Schafer. You have been most helpful.'

Schafer jumped out of the car. 'I'm not pleased to hear it,' he said and shutting the door he quickly vanished into the milling crowd of commuters.

On Thursday 30th November Ian and Schulz found themselves on the same flight from Berlin to Heathrow. They noticed each other as they boarded the Boeing 737. Ian could smell the stale tobacco on Schulz's coat and dropped back to put some distance between them. Ostensibly allowing a lady to board before him, Schulz heard the lady thanking Ian as she squeezed past him and watched as the rather smart young man helped her lift her baggage into the overhead locker.

On landing, both took the express train to King's Cross paying little attention to each other. From there, Ian headed for York and Schulz jumped into a taxi and asked to be taken to the Buckingham Palace end of The Mall. He then crossed The Mall and walked into St James's Park.

A man was leaning on some iron railings, feeding bread to the ducks and Schulz stopped beside him and watched as the ducks dived for the bread, fiercely competing for the one morsel thrown each time.

Simon Black had aged over the last two years but somehow looked more relaxed; he wore slightly more modern, horned-rimmed glasses and, perhaps as a self-defence mechanism for his impending retirement, was less intense. He was not, however, going to give up without a fight and luckily for him the hand of history had moved in his favour. Firstly, there had been the stirrings of the Polish trade-union movement, Solidarity, in January 1989 and Black had managed to convince the Foreign Office that he was receiving valuable traffic from behind the Iron Curtain and that he needed to stay on for "just a few months." Then, in May, the Hungarian government opened its borders with Austria resulting in thousands of East Germans taking their holidays in Hungary and ending up in the West. Finally, encouraged by Gorbachev, the Berlin Wall became a symbol of the past rather than a barrier to the future and with a new chief at MI6 and a new Foreign Secretary in Douglas Hurd, much to the annoyance of his boss and bête-noire, Rebecca Topping, his Cold War expertise had been considered crucial and his tenure had been extended for another year.

Black didn't look at Schulz but kept throwing bread, one piece at a time.

'How can I help you? Black asked with little enthusiasm.

Schulz turned towards him. 'I want to defect,' he replied. 'I have some sensitive information which I am willing to hand over.' His voice revealed some anxiety.

'And what do you want in return?' Black asked as he

took one pace sideways. His tone was flat, matter-of-fact.

'A flat in Chelsea and a generous pension for the rest of my life.'

'Don't we all!' Black scoffed.

There were similarities between these two intelligence officers but differences too. Neither were married, nor had they any children. Both were objective and cold but Schulz was also a sadist; Black was not. Schulz could show emotions, such as anger; for Black this was rare. Schulz could be impulsive; with Black, everything was planned.

'I have information that a Werner Hoffmann who worked for the Vatican Bank discovered the details of a high-ranking Nazi refugee, smuggled with the help of the Catholic Church to Britain. Hoffman died from food poisoning many years ago but before he died, I understand he sequestrated all the paperwork into a safe deposit box.' Schulz had made some assumptions here but knew his scant information needed padding out.

'You understand? You mean you don't have this information with you? Have you even seen it?' Black was being dismissive. It was standard procedure. By signifying that the information was not valuable the informant would be encouraged to reveal more in a desperate attempt to add value. Black just had to be careful, however, that he didn't push Schulz into fabricating the truth.

'I can get it,' Schulz replied. He was getting agitated and Black knew he had the upper hand.

'Anyway, why do you think we would be bothered about a Second World War Nazi? It's forty-four years since the War ended. He will be an old man by now, if he's still alive.'

Schulz was sweating but he knew he had to start fighting back.

'Because there must have been a reason why Britain gave him sanctuary and that reason may be embarrassing, if it comes out.' The implied threat in his voice was clear.

Black emptied the last of the breadcrumbs on the grass but still on the far side of the iron railings. 'Why should we pay you for this information? If this was sanctioned by the government, MI6 will already know the details.'

'MI6 might know but I doubt the British public do.' Schulz was being factual. He thought the information would be useful to MI6 but if they didn't want it someone would find it of value.

'So, we have to buy it or you will sell it to someone else?' Black looked at him for the first time. It was a look of disappointment, although it was all an act. He wanted as much information as possible for as little commitment as possible. 'I will have to see it first. Where is it now?'

'The information is in a bank vault in Rome,' Schulz replied, bluffing confidently.

'Well, you'd better go and get it.' Black's voice became high pitched at the end. He could almost have added the word *stupid*.

'When I have the documents in my hands, I will clarify the contents but I will not hand them over until we have an agreement.' Schulz was holding his ground.

Black thought for a few moments and then in a rather matter-of-fact sort of way said: 'Give me a call then, when you get back from Rome. When do you think that will be?'

'I have to obtain a pocket watch first, from Ireland. It contains the secret combination needed to open the safe deposit box but it is currently in the possession of a business woman.' Schulz had relaxed and immediately regretted giving too much away.

'And how do you propose to do that?' Black asked incredulously.

Schulz stared at Black. He had endured enough of his sarcasm.

'I have connections in Ireland,' he said, as he turned and walked away.

Chapter Six

It was now Monday the 4th December and having been away for a few days, Ian was intending to get in early and spend a full day in the office catching up, but he had only been at his desk a few minutes when Sarah put a call though from the niece of Tempest Huber.

'It's Mary James here. My uncle is in Ripon hospital and he says he wants a new Will. He's got a brain tumour and the doctor says he's not got long to live. I've also found a summons from the police for driving without tax and insurance.' She spoke quickly and was clearly stressed.

'All right. I will go and see him straight away,' Ian said trying to calm her down. 'Can you meet me at the hospital with the summons? I'll be there in about half an hour.'

'Yes, I'll go there now,' she said.

Ian sighed quietly to himself. Having to drive back to Ripon was the last thing he needed but with instructions like this he had to act immediately if he wanted to avoid a negligence claim. He grabbed the original Will out of the strongroom and made it to the hospital within 40 minutes. Mary was there to greet him. She looked prim and proper with short dark hair and an olive-skinned complexion.

'He's just through here,' she said pointing to a mixed ward of about a dozen patients.

'Okay, have you got the summons?'

'Yes, here,' she said passing it over.

Ian scanned the paperwork. 'He's meant to attend Ripon Magistrates Court on Wednesday but he obviously can't go. I will see if I can get a letter from his doctor.'

Ian turned to enter the ward and Mary started to follow.

'I'm sorry, I have to see him alone,' Ian said. 'There mustn't be any hint of undue influence or it could invalidate the Will.'

'I understand,' Mary replied.

Tempest was lying flat on the bed and he looked restless, moving his head from side to side.

'Hello, Mr Huber. Your niece asked me to come and see you. I understand you want to alter your Will?'

Tempest made no attempt to sit up but kept tossing his head from side-to-side. He looked feverish but was clearly trying to say something. Ian strained hard to decipher the words.

'I've got a son. Never recognised him. He's a taxi driver in Ripon. Bobby Baxter. Add him to Will. Split everything three ways,' was roughly what was said in between the restless movements.

Ian was uncomfortable. It was borderline as to whether Tempest had legal capacity to make a Will but although he was struggling to talk, he did seem to understand what he wanted.

'So, you're telling me you want to alter your Will so everything is split equally between your niece, your nephew and your son who is called Bobby Baxter?'

'Yes,' came the fevered reply.

'Okay, I will make the alterations to your Will now and you can sign it in a couple of minutes,' Ian said, his mind racing as he thought about the witnessing requirements.

Ian pulled the original Will out of the file and went to the clause dealing with the residuary estate. Where it said: "upon trust for such of them, my niece Mary James and my nephew Richard James in equal shares absolutely," Ian simply hand wrote "my son Bobby Baxter" before the reference to Mary. He then asked the matron if she would act as a witness and to his surprise she agreed. Perhaps, they were not as strict about such things in Ripon as Harrogate, he thought.

'Right, Mr Huber, I just need you to sign your name next to this alteration please.'

Tempest held the biro, still lying on his back and made his mark. Ian and the nurse signed with their full names and addresses and Ian dated the alteration.

'Okay, we're all done,' Ian said to Mary as he went to leave the hospital not telling her what the alteration was.

'What about the summons, Mr Sutherland? He only has a little white van for taking his chickens to shows and I think it will have just slipped his mind to renew the tax and insurance with him being poorly.'

'Don't worry about the Magistrates Court. I will sort something out,' Ian reassured her.

Ian asked the matron to get Mr Huber's doctor to telephone him and headed back to Harrogate.

Back in the office, Ian rang Angela.

'How did you get on in Berlin?' she asked anxiously.

'Well, I found Theo,' Ian replied. 'He's a Lutheran pastor now.'

'How is he?'

'He seemed well.'

'And what did he say?'

'Well, his mother is still alive and I think he feels some responsibility towards her and he has his congregation to look after so I don't think he wants to move far from Berlin.'

'Does he want to see me again?' Angela's voice was rising with every question.

'He asked after you and was pleased to hear of your success, and, yes, I think he would be happy to see you but there is something he wants to do first.'

'What's that?' Angela said sounding somewhat puzzled.

'I understand, just before you escaped, he gave you something called a deck watch and he would like it back to carry out some family research. Do you still have it?'

Angela paused for a second or two. 'Yes, it's in my jewellery box. I haven't looked at it in years.'

'Are you happy to let me have it so I can take it to him?'

'Er, yes but I wouldn't like to post it and I wasn't coming back to England anytime soon.' She clearly thought this a slightly strange request.

'I've thought about that. I fancy a trip to Dublin and I could bring my girlfriend with me and make a bit of a holiday of it, so I could meet you in Dublin if you like?'

'Okay, and you can give me a few more details when I see you. When can you come?

'I was thinking about this Friday but I will have to drive and get the ferry from Holyhead because we will have to bring our dog.'

'That's fine; there's no quarantine in Ireland. Why don't you come about five o'clock as it will take you most of the day to get here? We live at a house called An Diadan on Northumberland Road.'

'Excellent; I'll see you then but just one more thing,' Ian said letting out a gentle laugh. 'I must try a proper pint of Guinness. It's meant to be much better in Dublin. Can you recommend a traditional pub where I can get the genuine article?'

'I'll ask my husband,' Angela replied.

Sophie needed little convincing to take a short break in Dublin especially when Ian said they could take Sky.

Sophie had sold her Beetle when she moved to England because it was left hand drive and she had purchased a second-hand Mercedes 350 SL in a cream colour with a folding fabric, soft top roof cover and red leather seats. It was really a two-seater but there was a bench seat at the rear which Sky could lie across and plenty of room in the boot for luggage.

Ian had chosen the Friday because it was the last day of the Michaelmas term at Durham University and he thought it would be a nice way for Sophie to start her Christmas holidays. Firstly, however, he had to sort out Tempest's little problem in the Magistrates Court. It was, in fact surprisingly easy. Ian explained the situation, handed over the letter from the doctor which stated Tempest Huber would be unlikely to survive another week and the case was discharged. The preparations for Dublin were on!

Aidan O'Sullivan was a retired academic. Aged sixty-three his hair was silver grey and he wore it long and brushed back. He was slim and a little under six foot. His attire was trendy, smart-casual and he considered himself quite a dandy. As a young lecturer he had been a bit of a ladies' man but as an older husband he had always been faithful to Angela.

He was left wing, like many in his profession and, as an Irish rebel at heart, he had coupled this with a dislike of all things English. He had, therefore, been quite willing, when approached by the Stasi in the early 1960's, to provide little bits of information regarding his work in public international law at the Free University in West Berlin. He didn't think it was very significant. Just the comings and goings of politicians and personnel from NGOs. It was really just a matter of letting the Stasi know the sort of subjects the policy makers were thinking about; but it was quite exciting and made him feel important. In return he was welcomed as a visiting lecturer at Humboldt University in East Berlin where he was able to espouse his alternative views to the capitalist system.

Having struck up a relationship with Angela, however, he wanted her freedom and to his surprise the Stasi were willing to grant it. They felt it would give him a better cover to be partnered with an East German refugee so when he tentatively mentioned her intended escape, they were willing to look the other way. He had panicked at the last minute and also informed them that Theo would be in the back of the car, in case Theo was discovered and he was held to blame. The Stasi were, it seemed, even willing to turn a blind eye towards Theo but then the guard spotted the suitcases and it all went wrong. Angela knew nothing of this and it was all a long time ago. Since he had come back to Ireland virtually all communication with the Stasi had ceased and it was a part of his life that he had put to the back of his mind. To the Stasi, however, he was a sleeper and he was about to find out that there was no such thing as a free lunch.

When his telephone rang Aidan answered it with his usual cheerful bonhomie but as soon as he heard the voice of Peter Schulz his heart sank. After some brief pleasantries

Schulz began:

'I believe your wife left Berlin with a watch given to her by her fiancé? You are probably not aware of this?' Schulz had a way with words that always brought back unwanted memories.

Aidan had been caught off guard but he managed a coherent, if somewhat hesitant reply.

'Well, yes, actually, I am. Funnily enough, she's just received a telephone call about it. An English lawyer is coming here to collect it from her the day after tomorrow.'

'Really?' Schulz replied, hardly able to believe his luck. 'And why is that?'

Aidan wondered where to begin.

'When the Wall came down, my wife hired a lawyer to go and find Theo Hoffman and, surprisingly, he did! He's just got back from Berlin and apparently, Hoffman wants his watch back for some family research, whatever that means. I suppose it must have some sentimental value.'

There was an awkward silence whilst Schulz thought things through.

'What do you want with it?' Aidan asked interrupting Schulz's train of thought.

'It has an unusual significance.'

'Do you want me to get it for you?' Aidan was becoming anxious.

'No,' Schulz said firmly. 'What is the name of this lawyer?'

'I think Angela said he is called Ian Sutherland.'

'Let him have the watch. We will get it off him. That way Angela will not be alerted to anything out of the ordinary. It would look strange if it went missing from your house.'

'Right, so I don't need to do anything?' Aidan asked somewhat relieved.

'Not quite. After he has collected the watch let me know where he is going.'

'I think I can tell you now,' Aidan said feeling like a good boy and hoping for a pat on the back. 'He's coming here about 5 o'clock and then going for a pint of Guinness. I've been asked to recommend an authentic bar so I was going to suggest Hogan's. It has the best Guinness in town.'

'That is most helpful. Telephone me when Sutherland leaves the house. If I need anything else I'll let you know,' Schulz replied, sending a chill down Aidan's spine.

It took three and a half hours to drive to Anglesey and it was quite a rush to make the 10.00am ferry. Ian and Sophie gave Sky a little breather before they embarked because then there would be another three-and-a-half-hour journey before they reached Dublin and at this time of year the Irish Sea could be rough.

'I hope she's not sick in the back of the car,' Ian said.

'Oh, that's why you wanted to come in my Mercedes is it!' Sophie exclaimed.

Northumberland Road was a major thoroughfare and

the house was a substantial Georgian semi, set well back from the road. Built of red brick behind black, wrought-iron railings it had broad steps leading up to the front doorway which had arched, patterned brick work. To the left were two large sash windows and upstairs, there were three, all symmetrically spaced. Below the steps, half above ground level and half below this pattern was repeated in the basement and to the right of the steps was a driveway and garage.

As Ian stood at the door and knocked, he realised the house was clearly making a statement. It was a house for the Irish gentry; the well-off, powerful and educated members of society. Exactly, the sort of place you would expect to find a left-wing, university professor.

Angela answered the door.

'Hello, Ian. Do come in,' and then she looked behind him and said: 'I thought you were bringing your girlfriend?'

'She's just gone to walk the dog. We're going to meet up again in half an hour.'

Angela took Ian down the hall, into a modern kitchen which overlooked a walled garden to the rear.

'What would you like to drink?'

'Coffee please.'

Angela filled a cafetiere with boiling water and whilst the coffee was brewing, she handed Ian the watch, wrapped in a soft black cloth.

'Here you are. Exactly as Theo handed it to me all those

years ago.'

Ian opened up the cloth and held the watch in his hand. There was nothing unusual about it. It was silver with a swastika on the back of the case.

'So, tell me a bit more about him. How was he?' Angela asked, as she moved around the kitchen, putting some milk on the cooker to warm and reaching for some porcelain mugs from the top of a cupboard.

'Well, after he was caught, he was interrogated and beaten-up by the Stasi. Then he went to prison for about two years. I think that changed him and limited his options for employment when he came out. He said the church was somewhat anti-establishment and welcomed free thinkers so he became a Lutheran pastor. He's now based at St Mary's and seems fairly content with his lot.'

Ian was looking at the watch as he spoke and popped open the back. Angela noticed.

'And why does he want the watch?'

'Something to do with his father's death, I think,' Ian replied distractedly.

'Theo said it was his father's. I suppose it has sentimental value.'

Ian was still looking inside the watch. Inscribed on the movement it said: "A. Lange & Sohne, Glashutte I-SA and there was a number, 204732. So, it is just the maker's name and serial number. Not much of a clue there, Ian thought.

Angela handed Ian his coffee just as Aidan entered the

kitchen.

'Mr Sutherland, I presume?' he said holding out his hand. Ian assumed he must have come in from outside because he was wearing a long, Donegal tweed coat and scarf over dark red cords and an Aran sweater.

'Yes,' Ian said standing up and shaking his hand which he noticed was unpleasantly clammy. 'How do you do?'

'I understand you want me to recommend a good place for a Guinness?

'Yes, please. I understand it's much better in Ireland?'

'And even better in Dublin! Guinness doesn't travel well. Hogan's is where you want to go, just this side of Trinity College. Walk straight down Northumberland Road towards town and you will see it opposite College Park.'

'Thank you,' Ian replied.

'Right, I'll let you two to get on with your business,' Aidan said as he turned to leave.

Ian thought Aidan was going to take himself off to the sitting room or somewhere else in the house but he heard the front door shut so he must have been on his way out when he introduced himself.

Ian answered Angela's further questions as best as he could and agreed to contact her again when he returned from Berlin.

Sophie was waiting outside for him so they immediately set off in the Mercedes towards Trinity College. Ian carefully placed the deck watch, wrapped in its cloth, in the glovebox of the car and as he lifted his head, he spotted Aidan by a parade of shops just coming out of a phone box. It was like an English one but painted green and Ian thought it a little odd because there was clearly a telephone in the house.

Hogan's was easy to find, situated as it was on the corner of the main road. Sophie turned left and pulled up at the side of the pub, leaving Sky in the car and the windows slightly open.

'I won't ask you what you want to drink because you have to have a pint of Guinness,' Ian said laughing.

'It's not very ladylike,' Sophie objected half-heartedly.

'For Guinness, we can make an exception,' Ian said smiling at her as he stood back to let her enter first.

Ian went to the bar and ordered two pints of Guinness. The barman was small, very slim and probably in his early sixties. His head was shaved leaving little more than a shadow of grey hair at the back and sides and he appeared nervous. Very nervous.

'You have a seat and I will bring them over,' he said, pointing to one of the empty tables, as the pints had to be pulled and settle before being ready to drink.

Ian noticed they were being stared at. He felt as though they had just entered someone's sitting room, uninvited. Nevertheless, he and Sophie sat at a little wooden table by a roaring log fire and after a few minutes the barman brought over two pints of Guinness, so they started to relax.

'Thank you,' Ian said holding up his glass and admiring the contents.

Ian drew a heart shape in the creamy head on the top of Sophie's glass with his little finger.

'Ah, that's sweet,' she said.

'I'm not being sweet; I'm just checking it's the right consistency!' Ian teased.

Sophie gave him a seductive smile. 'I see I have a lot to learn about this drink,' she said.

Neither of them had been to Ireland before. It was dark and damp outside and they were enjoying the warmth of the fire despite feeling like intruders. Suddenly, the barman came up beside Ian and whispered in his ear.

'There's going to be trouble. Quick you'd better come out the back,' he said visibly shaking. He looked deadly nervous.

'What sort of trouble?' Ian asked, slightly bemused.

'It's FADA. They've been marching and we're the next stop on their route. They won't take kindly to you English.'

Ian remembered something being in the news about a march a few months ago. The Forum for a Democratic Alternative had organised a march on the British Embassy in Ballsbridge at which Gerry Adams had addressed a crowd of about 15,000 people. He had called for an island free of British military occupation and free of partition. Ian had always thought of *the troubles* as being in Northern Ireland but Ballsbridge was just up the road and it was also the location of their hotel, the InterContinental.

He stood up but something made him hesitate. They could be walking into a trap but he had to make a snap decision and there was no reason not to trust the barman. In fact, he seemed genuinely worried on their behalf.

'Quickly, this way,' the barman said.

Sophie gave Ian a worried look but he indicated that she should follow. The barman took them behind the bar through a small kitchen and then opened a thick oak door which led into a courtyard. It was dark and there were no outside lights on but Ian could see by the light from the kitchen that it was bounded by a six-foot cobble wall on all three sides. It was drizzling and there was a blanket of clouds. Ian could see a large square shape in the corner and realised it was an oil tank. Again, he hesitated.

'There's a door in the side there which leads into the street. Go quickly,' the barman urged, pointing at the doorway in the wall diagonally across from them.

They stepped into the courtyard and the barman shut the kitchen door behind them. Ian heard the sound of the door being locked and his heart sank. For a moment, you could have heard a pin drop.

Out of the gloom from behind the oil tank two figures appeared. The first was a tallish man with a short white beard. He was wearing a dark Brooklyn cap and a dark coat and he looked to be in his late fifties. The second man was much younger; perhaps thirty-five. He had dark brown hair and a lighter, more ginger coloured beard which looked a little unusual. He was holding a shillelagh across his body, with the handle in his right hand and the gnarled knob resting in the palm of his left. For some reason, Ian assumed they were father and son.

'We've come for the watch,' the older one said. 'Hand it over and you can go without any trouble.'

Ian's mind started to race. 'It's in the car,' he replied.

The older man gestured with his hand as though to say "after you" and Ian headed towards the doorway, slowly, turning back to look at Sophie as he did so. Sophie tried to follow him but the younger man stepped up behind her and trapped her neck between the shillelagh and his chest.

'You're staying with me missy,' he said as she let out a scream.

Instantly, Ian exploded into action and charged at the younger man. He grabbed the shillelagh with both hands and pushed it over Sophie's head so she was able to get out of the way. The younger man was stumbling backwards with the force of Ian's momentum but he managed to stay on his feet. Ian tried to hold on to the shillelagh but as they scrambled with each other it fell to the floor and both men looked down as it hit the concrete.

Quickly, Ian hit Sophie's assailant with a right hook and winced as his knuckles made contact with the man's cheekbone. Sophie was still in-between Ian and the older man, who stooped to pick up the shillelagh, but Sophie flung herself at him grabbing the lapel of his coat. Without hesitation, he threw her to his side smacking her in the mouth as she fell.

Ian and the younger man were still in close combat as the older man seized the shillelagh. They were gripping on to each other's clothes as the younger man continued his backwards journey towards the wall opposite the doorway.

Suddenly, Ian felt the force of the shillelagh across his shoulder and the top of his back but the impact was askew and he was able to ignore the pain as the two men parried blows. Then a second blow came but this time both men had twisted and it seemed to make contact with both of them across the sides of their arms. Ian was desperately thinking what to do about the older man behind him but he had not yet overpowered the younger one. He glanced behind and saw Sophie taking a second run at his attacker but the man grabbed her by the wrist and hurled her against the back wall.

Ian wanted to break off. Wanted to change from one hitman to the next but he was still held by the younger man. With a supreme effort he broke free and landed a full-length punch right on the man's nose. He dropped like a stone; his arms outstretched, just as a third hit from the shillelagh made target. This time the older man's aim was better. He had swung the shillelagh in a huge semi-circle from above his head straight into Ian's side.

Ian screamed out loud as the air was forced from his

lung. He collapsed on the floor, gasping for breath. He was in agony and shocked by the pain. The blow must have broken some ribs. He was worried he may have punctured a lung but there was no blood coming from his mouth. He put a hand on the ground in the press-up position to lift himself but his strength was gone. He looked up as the older man lifted the shillelagh above his head. There was nothing he could do. He was out of time.

For a moment, he thought the coup de grace was coming but Sky had heard the commotion. Locked in the car she had been jumping from back to front and back again desperately trying to get out. She had scratched madly at the windows. The rear window was made of plastic and her claws slit through the material like a stiletto as she burst through the opening with the force of a rocket.

Ian saw her leaping over the wall and with one bound, she flew at his assailant. She bit him on the backside and he screamed out in pain, turning around to try and hit her with the shillelagh but Sky grabbed his arm and the more he tried to shake her off the more she pulled back sinking her teeth in as she did so. It was actually quite terrifying to watch.

Ian could see her baring her teeth as she shook the older man from side to side. He was screaming in terror. For a few seconds Ian let her have her way but then he worried she might do the man some serious injury. By now Ian had regained just enough strength to get up and grabbing Sky's collar he pulled her away.

'Good girl,' he gasped.

The older man dropped to his knees and Ian saw he had wet himself.

Still holding Sky, he staggered over to Sophie and helped her up. Her bottom lip was swollen and bleeding and her eyes were full of tears.

'Are you okay? he asked holding her hand. Sophie nodded.

'Right, let's get out of here,' he said and they ran to the car.

could be pulled her away.

'Good grief,' he gasped.

The older man dropped to his knees and Ian saw he had wet himself.

still holding Skye he staggered over to Sophie and helped her up, her bottom lip was swollen and bleeding

Chapter Seven

Ian and Sophie jumped into the Mercedes and Ian followed the signs for St James's Hospital which was not too far away. Sophie's lower lip was swollen and bloody and she held a handkerchief against her face to hide her embarrassment. Ian's side was bearable if he was careful how he moved but he was worried he had broken some ribs.

Ian wanted Sophie to be attended to first but in the Accident and Emergency department the triage process saw Ian taken away to a separate area where he was examined by a young doctor who exuded confidence.

'I slipped getting out of the bath,' Ian explained, hoping the other battle scars were not too obvious.

'It looks like you may have cracked a rib or two but there is no treatment necessary. Just rest and take things carefully for a few weeks. There is no serious damage,' the doctor assured him.

'Don't you need to X-ray me?' Ian asked somewhat surprised.

'No, as I say, everything is in the right place and rest is all you need. Take some paracetamol if you are in pain.'

'How long until they mend?' Ian continued still concerned at the lack of information.

'Six weeks probably but you will feel better much quicker than that. Just be careful for a while.'

'Okay,' Ian replied as he got up and went in search of Sophie.

Sophie was sat in the waiting area. A nurse had cleaned her wound and apart from a bit of a swelling and cut to the lip she was fine.

'Good to go?' Ian asked.

'Yes. Just get me back to the hotel.'

They hurried to the Mercedes and headed for their hotel in Ballsbridge.

'I wonder who was behind that?' Ian said, trying to understand why they had been attacked.

'I don't know who it could be,' Sophie replied. 'Someone must have known you had collected the watch and instructed those thugs to get it off you. In fact, they must have known you were going to collect it because otherwise there wouldn't be time to organise the ambush.'

'Only Angela and Aidan knew I had collected the watch and only they knew I was going to collect it.'

'Do you suspect them?' Sophie asked raising her voice in surprise.

'I suspect him. He left the house before me and as we drove past that parade of shops, I saw him coming out of a phone box. Why would he use a phone box when they have a phone in the house?'

Sophie thought for a moment. 'Because he didn't want his wife to hear?'

'Exactly! I think he's up to something but why would he want the watch? It doesn't really make sense. I don't think Angela will know what he's doing but I'm going to be very careful from now on. I'm not going to trust either of them.'

'Can't you just abandon this job now?' Sophie pleaded. 'You've found Theo. You're always putting yourself in danger.'

'I want to see it through and I agreed to take the watch to Theo in Berlin but I'll wrap things up soon. Something isn't right,' Ian replied, whilst still trying to work out what it was.

The InterContinental hotel had a grand entrance and spacious reception but Ian and Sophie did not want to linger so they hurried up to their bedroom with Sky in tow. Ian settled her down on a car rug in the corner of the bedroom whilst Sophie showered, then, as Sophie dried her hair, Ian showered.

With a towel around his waist, Ian looked in the mirror and combed back his hair. One of his eyelids was swollen so he soaked a flannel in cold water, got some ice from the mini-bar and then lay on the bed with the flannel over his eyes. A few minutes rest will do me good, he thought, as he replayed the events of the day in his mind over and over again.

Ian could hear Sophie in the background. The hairdryer stopped, there was a final brush of the hair and then there was the opening of drawers and the sound of steps as presumably, Sophie unpacked her suitcase.

She was getting dressed. Ian could tell she was getting dressed because he heard the bath towel being thrown in the bath and the sound of press studs. He wondered what she was wearing as Ian was hoping for a quiet night in with room service and thought she would just put on her pyjamas.

He then heard the sound of make-up. A lipstick being placed back on the dressing table and the scent of perfume being sprayed. It was Coco Chanel and it was Ian's favourite scent because he associated it with Sophie.

Ian was going to have to make a move. It looked as though Sophie wanted to go down for dinner but then he heard her go back into the bathroom. Perhaps she wants to use the larger mirror, Ian thought, as he decided to have another few minutes rest.

Then he heard the click of high heels on the tiled floor. He found it vaguely arousing although this feeling was mixed with a slight reluctance to make the effort to dress for dinner.

Neither of them had spoken for several minutes but now Ian heard Sophie coming towards him. His adrenalin had dissipated after the stress of the fight but Sophie was buzzing. Her fear in the courtyard had turned to elation that they had departed the victors and she found her man deeply attractive.

She straddled him on the bed and grabbing his wrists she pushed them above his head.

'Now you are all mine,' she joked with a menacing tone in her voice.

Ian shook the flannel off his face and looked at Sophie in wonder. She was wearing a black corset which was tight around the waist and accentuated her breasts, sheer black stockings and her black stilettos.

Sophie's bottom lip was still swollen but she had covered it with lipstick and she leant forward to kiss Ian gently on his swollen eyelid. He winced slightly as she lunged forward because she still had his arms behind his head and the movement stretched his ribs.

The towel loosened and she pulled it from under him. On this occasion she was taking control. She let Ian bend his arms but with his hands still either side of his head she pressed down on them as she slowly moved herself up and down, giving him little kisses as she did so.

Suddenly she sat upright and Ian placed his hands on her waist as she gasped and groaned and dug her fingers into his chest. Then she collapsed on top of him. Ian wrapped his arms around her and for a few minutes they just lay in each other's arms.

Sky started to whine and stood up wagging her tail,

looking anxious. Ian knelt down and gave her a thorough stroke on both sides of her neck.

'Good girl,' he said. 'I will order you some room service.'

'I thought you were talking to me then,' Sophie joked.

'You can have room service too,' Ian replied smiling back at her.

Ian ordered sirloin steak, chips and salad to be brought to the room with a bottle of St Emilion.

They ate their sirloins cutting off the back fat for Sky and then took her for a last walk around Herbert Park. It was a cold night with a clear sky speckled with a sprinkling of stars but as they meandered hand in hand along the footpaths nothing became clear. Forty odd years ago, Werner Hoffmann had said an important Nazi was moving to Britain with the help of the Catholic Church. His watch held a secret. Ian had collected it and now they had been attacked. Who was behind this and why? Ian had no idea.

The next morning there was just time for a little Christmas shopping and Ian took Sophie into Brown Thomas, the department store. Sophie admired some Christmas tree ornaments of animals so Ian bought them for her. She chose a penguin, a polar bear and a goose. They came out of the Grafton Street entrance and wandered, accidentally, straight up to Weir & Sons, the jewellers. Sophie stopped and looked at the rings in the window. Her mind was settled upon making a nest and she pointed out the ones she liked but Ian didn't take the hint.

Home late that night and then into work early the following Monday morning, Ian was stressed. He was spending too much time out of the office and he felt permanently behind the curve but as soon as he was in, Sarah ruined his day.

'Mr Huber has been on the telephone and he wants you to visit him. He wants a new Will.'

'What!' Ian exclaimed. 'I thought he was about to die.'

'Well, he's at home now and he wants to see you.'

'Did he telephone himself?' Ian asked.

'Yes. Oh, and by the way, Hannah has put a meeting in your diary with her and Steve Fell for eleven o'clock in the Boardroom.'

'What's that about?'

'I've no idea,' Sarah replied in a way which revealed she didn't care either.

Ian was calm and relaxed as he sat at the head of the Boardroom table with Hannah sat immediately to his right and Steve a little further up to his left.

Ian's psyche was, he hadn't done anything wrong so he had nothing to worry about or so he thought, but his absences had given his enemies room to manoeuvre.

Ryders didn't really have an agricultural department but in so far as it did, Ian was head of it. He had a sort of farming background as his father had worked for a large animal feeds business after the War and following his death

Ian's mother had bought a farmhouse and fifty acres as a hobby farm. So, Ian understood the business of farming and had a good rapport with farmers.

'Thank you for coming, Ian. You're probably wondering what this is all about?' Hannah said looking apprehensive.

'Yes,' Ian replied.

'I wanted to ask you, who you think is best suited to run the rural department now that we want to accelerate its expansion?' She emphasized the word *rural*.

Ian looked puzzled. He already was head of the agricultural department. 'Well, me, of course.'

'Well, we don't think so,' Steve interjected. 'You think it should be called the *agricultural department* and we think it should be called *Ryders Rural*. It's far more encompassing.'

Ian was taken aback. Steve's tone was aggressive. It was as though there had been an argument over this issue which there hadn't.

'I'm not set on any name,' Ian replied. 'It is just that the non-agricultural work which you consider *rural*, fits into other categories as well. You've mentioned Wills and business advice and family law for country folk but if they want such advice, they won't look for *rural lawyers*. Farmers on the other hand, will look for *agricultural lawyers* and, in any case, I thought it was the large farming businesses which we were after?'

'Well, you haven't done anything to get them. You're

never here!' Steve was on the attack which surprised Ian as they had never had a cross word although they didn't particularly like each other.

'I was told to take things slowly as the partnership had not decided if it wanted to be known for this specialism or not,' Ian retorted as he turned towards Hannah for support. It was not forthcoming and as the debate continued, with Ian remaining calm and Steve on the attack, Hannah remained silent – a silence which indicated both her approval and her prior knowledge of what was taking place.

'Well, we think Steve would be best placed to take this forward,' Hannah said eventually.

Ian was still struggling to take this in. Steve knew nothing about farming and only had one or two farming clients who had litigation issues.

'I don't think this is the right decision,' Ian countered. 'It should, at least, be discussed at a full partners' meeting.'

Hannah relented probably because it relieved her of some of the responsibility.

'Very well', she said. 'We'll put in on the next Agenda.'

Furious with the shenanigans going on behind his back, after a brief trip into town for a sandwich, Ian headed back to his desk to eat his lunch. Just as he started to calm down a little Mark Thompson wandered in.

'How's you?' His tone was mild and almost friendly. Ian was immediately suspicious because he would definitely know about the land grab made by Steve Fell.

"Yes, fine thanks.'

'I've got a new client for you. Hayden Boyes. He's selling a penthouse flat on Beech Grove overlooking The Stray. I've given him your name. His father's Ernest Boyes of BCI so you'd better look after him.'

'Do you mean BCI as in British Chemical Industries?'

'That's the one. Play this right and we could get a lot more business.'

BCI was a large private chemical business in Leeds that had invented a special type of black paint. It was especially tough and chip resistant so was used on outdoor surfaces such as the iron work on bridges. However, it was also the darkest substance known to man with unrivalled absorption of light throughout the range from ultra violet through to infrared. The ultra-low reflectance gave it some special qualities so it could be used for certain military purposes such as camouflage. Obviously, the owners had made a fortune.

'I thought they would have Leeds solicitors,' Ian replied.

'They do, but Hayden lives in Harrogate and Fentons recommended us for the conveyancing,' Mark said referring to the up-market estate agents.

'And Fentons gave him your name?' Ian asked somewhat surprised as they had more contact with Ian than Thompson.

'Yes, Steve and I had lunch with them earlier in the week.'

'Oh, I see,' Ian replied a little taken aback. 'Well, yes, of course, I will look after him.'

'Thanks,' was all Mark actually said as he turned and left Ian's office but to himself he was saying, 'mission accomplished.'

Steaming with anger, Ian drove to Ripon to see Tempest Huber. He didn't really like him and was worrying about what he had told the Magistrates who had discharged the case on the grounds that Mr Huber was terminally ill and, according to his doctor, unlikely to survive the week. Regardless of this, however, Ian had a professional duty to give a timely service so he pushed the Jag hard through the corners as he worked off his frustration whilst at the same time being careful not to let his mood affect the safety of his driving.

Another shock awaited Ian on his arrival at the smallholding. All the hen huts had gone. There was no livestock on site and the land had been completely cleared. A few smouldering fires glowed in the afternoon gloom and wisps of smoke lingered in the damp air.

Ian found Tempest sat in his usual place in the kitchen.

'Hello, Mr Huber. How are you?'

'I've been better,' Tempest replied gruffly.

'What's happened outside?' Ian asked getting straight to the point.

'My nephew, Richard, has destroyed everything. He's got rid of all my prize livestock and burnt all my sheds. There's nothing left.'

'Why would he do that?'

'Because he didn't think I was coming back!' Tempest's face was going red with anger. 'But I surprised them all you see. I discharged myself. The hospital tried to stop me and said I wouldn't be able to get up the stairs but I showed them my walking stick and said I can hook the handle around the spindles on the staircase and hoist myself up.' Tempest picked up his stick and gave Ian a demonstration. Ian had to admire his determination.

'Well, I'm glad to see you so well. Now how can I help you?'

Tempest's voice became even gruffer than usual. 'I want a new Will. Take this down. I want it to say: "I leave £1 to Richard James for the burning of and damage to good property whilst I was in hospital."'

Ian wasn't surprised that Richard James was getting the chop but he was worried about the suggested wording.

'So, are you telling me you want to change your Will to leave £1 to Richard James and then split the residue between your niece and son equally?'

'Yes, but you have to put in that wording,' Tempest said, repeating it.

'Right, I will have to check that is okay. I've never done anything like that before but I'll make the changes and come back as soon as I can.'

Ian went back to the office and asked Hannah about it. It was easy enough to delete the reference to the nephew but to actually leave him £1 and deliver a reprimand seemed a bit malicious even if the nephew had jumped the gun.

'If they are his instructions you will have to follow them,' Hannah replied. 'There's nothing illegal about it.'

'Okay, and oh, I was a bit surprised by our meeting this morning. It seemed rather pre-meditated.'

'You're right it should be discussed more widely. You will get your opportunity,' she said, as she turned back to her desk and looked at some papers.

The next day Ian went back to Mr Huber's to get the new Will signed. Ian was relieved that a new Will had been retyped and would be signed normally without the alterations of the last copy. He was also relieved that all the livestock had gone because he was taking one of the secretaries Debbie with him and at least the farmstead was a little less toxic.

The visit was straight forward but, on the journey back, Debbie unburdened her concerns.

'Did you know Tracy and Cheryl have been given a salary increase?' she asked.

'No!' Ian replied with alarm.

'Yes, apparently, she just walked into Mark's office and he said, "I'm giving you and Cheryl a rise as you work harder than the others."'

'He can't do that. It's a partnership decision,' Ian retorted.

'Well, the rest of us are a bit upset about it actually. We all work hard and it makes us think we aren't appreciated.'

'I'm not surprised. Leave it with me; I'll look into it,' Ian reassured her.

In Berlin, Peter Schulz had been putting off his call to Simon Black but he knew he had to make it. Things were moving fast. The Stasi were shredding files as quickly as they could and he wanted to defect before the recriminations started. All O'Sullivan had to do was arrange the collection of a watch off a small-town lawyer using a couple of local thugs and somehow, he had managed to bungle it.

'Simon Black speaking,' Black said as he picked up the telephone in his office.

'Hello. It's Peter Schulz.'

'How can I help you?' Black replied. Schulz thought this was strange. It was as though their conversation in the park had never taken place. Maybe that was the point, Schulz thought. Perhaps, Black is worried about being overheard.

'I'm afraid there will be some delay in providing the information,' Schulz said discretely. 'We encountered a problem in Dublin.'

'I'm sorry to hear that. Can you remedy it?'

'The item we are after is now in the hands of an English

lawyer. We don't know his whereabouts but we think he will return to Berlin to meet the subject and then we will retrieve it. It should just be a short delay.'

There was a brief silence as Black pondered.

'I don't suppose you know the name of this lawyer, do you?' he asked.

'We believe he is called Ian Sutherland but we have no other information about him.'

There was another silence at the other end of the line. If Schulz could have seen Black, he would have seen a man sit back in his chair and smile. He didn't show any teeth but the smile was broad.

'Are you there?' Schulz asked disturbing Black's thoughts.

'Yes, I'm here. This is getting interesting. Keep me informed,' he said as he hung up the phone.

Black always had a plan B; never relied on anyone and never trusted anyone. He liked to mix things up. He liked playing games; to set hares running to see what happened. He justified this by believing that somehow this allowed every opportunity to play out and fate would bring about the best solution.

He picked up the telephone and rang a number at the Vatican. Monsignor Demarco Marchetti answered. He was a middle-aged man with oval, silver-rimmed glasses. Fully robed and wearing a skull cap you could only see his face which had a permanent look of disapproval. He was a severe man; uncompromising and dogmatic. He was also head of VIS – the Vatican Information Service.

Hardly anyone had heard of the VIS and that is how the Vatican liked it but Vatican City was a sovereign state and it had all those institutions that other states possessed. Ostensibly, the VIS was meant to have charitable purposes but, allegedly, it was little different from any other intelligence service although perhaps less accountable.

After the usual professional pleasantries Black commenced:

'I am aware that just after the War a whistle-blower called Werner Hoffman stole some information from the Vatican Bank.' Black used the word "stole" to indicate he was making a friendly approach.

'I vaguely remember hearing something about this years ago,' Monsignor Demarco replied 'but, as far as I can recall, nothing ever surfaced.'

'No, he died of food poisoning. I suppose the assumption was the information died with him.' Black's words were cutting and Monsignor Demarco was unsettled by them.

'Yes, well this was all a long time ago. What is your interest after all this time?' Monsignor Demarco asked with obvious irritation.

'Oh, just a common courtesy,' Black lied. 'We have some information from our contacts in Berlin that Hoffmann's son, Theo, and an English lawyer, a man called Ian Sutherland, have the details of a safe deposit box in Rome and they are on their way to find out what's in it. Apparently, the secret combination to unlock the safe deposit box is contained in a deck watch which Sutherland has just collected from Dublin.'

'Safe deposit boxes don't have combinations. They are operated by two keys; at least they are in Rome,' Demarco said dismissively.

This caught Black unawares. He hadn't really thought of the practicalities but he suspected Demarco was right.

'Well, I just thought I should forewarn you, that's all,' Black said after a slight pause. 'We don't want the information getting into the wrong hands, do we?'

Black put the phone down and swivelled his chair around so he could look out over the Thames. Monsignor Demarco had a point about the combination lock. The story didn't quite stack up. It was still incomplete. Nevertheless, he was happy. The game was becoming more interesting and Ian Sutherland was his favourite toy.

Chapter Eight

Sophie wasn't too pleased when Ian said he was going back to Berlin and she was concerned about the partnership issues. She wanted security for Ian and for herself and it appeared as though things were moving in the wrong direction. There was no point trying to dissuade him, however, so after flying from Manchester Airport on the Wednesday, Thursday morning saw Ian back in Alexanderplatz sipping coffee with Theo.

Ian slid the watch across the table and Theo opened the back. He was struggling to concentrate because he felt disturbed by the information Ian had just given him about the events in Dublin. He also felt a little responsible and was worried that he was putting Ian in danger.

'I just can't make any sense of it,' Theo said. 'All it says is: "A. LANGE & SOHNE GLASHUTTE I-SA and the number 204732." All Lange & Sohne deck watches will say the same. How can this be a key to some incredible mystery?'

Ian wrote the inscription down carefully in a notebook and then started playing about with the letters. He kept writing down different words whilst Theo rambled on about maybe it was all a mistake and the secret documents, if there were any, had been lost when his father died.

Ian was only half listening as he re-arranged the letters and crossed out the corresponding letter in the inscription above. He was also trying to form words that could actually mean something in terms of a clue.

'I keep getting the words glass and house,' Ian said, sort of to himself but loudly enough for Theo to hear. Then, at the same time as Theo said 'what?' Ian said, 'and angel.'

'Could it be something to do with an angel in a glasshouse?' Ian asked. Theo just looked puzzled as he tried to find an association.

'I've got to use all the letters,' Ian said, his head still down as he crossed out one letter and scribbled down another. Eventually, he lifted up his head and said:

'At the house in a glass angel. Does that mean anything to you?'

For the second time in their brief relationship, Theo looked as if he had seen a ghost.

'It's an anagram,' Ian continued. 'Do you know of a house with a glass angel?'

'Yes,' Theo replied hesitantly. 'My father's house just outside Rome. It belongs to the church. It's set in beautiful gardens and at the end of the drive, near the entrance, is an art deco, stained glass sculpture of an angel, pointing towards heaven.'

Both men stared at each other for a moment. Eventually,

Ian broke the silence.

'We need to go to Rome.'

However, after some discussion, they realised it could not be an immediate trip. Ian had a return flight to Manchester booked and Theo's diary was getting filled up by Christmas events at St Mary's.

'On second thoughts you don't need me,' Ian said sliding the watch across the table. 'My job is done as they say. You could go on your own.'

'I think you have just shown you are part of this story now Ian,' Theo replied pushing the watch back to him. 'I'd like you to come, and keep the watch for now; it's safer with you. Let's stay in touch and maybe when we meet up in Rome you could bring Angela with you. She will like Rome.'

'Okay but it will have to be after Christmas. How about early January?' Ian asked after some thought.

'Yes, it's my busiest time of year too. We'll wait until after Epiphany.'

'I feel I've just had one!' Ian said as he drained the last dregs of his coffee and made haste. 'Cheerio. I've got to go and see some lawyers about restitution of property.'

Theo gave a knowing smile; as though he was thinking that Angela would not want to miss out on that opportunity.

The offices of Albrecht Berger & Co were a modern 1960s creation of concrete with aluminium window frames and a grey exterior. They were functional with no architectural merit but the building still had a significant presence. Inside, the reception area was similarly stark but the ladies on the front desk were efficient and the overall impression was one of professionalism.

Ian was taken in the lift to one of the upper floors where Ingrid Stein greeted him in a smaller reception area taking him from there to a glass walled meeting room.

She was tall with dark hair and glasses. She had come highly recommended by a London firm Ian had connections with and Ian could immediately see why. She exuded confidence, in a reassuring way, and this confidence obviously stemmed from her self-awareness of her own intelligence. She was fluent in four languages; German, English, French and Dutch, she practised law internationally and she read all the European newspapers before work, so she was as well versed on Margaret Thatcher's views on reunification as those of Helmut Kohl.

'Welcome to Albrecht Berger, Mr Sutherland. We are looking forward to helping you.'

She looked slightly flustered. Like someone just coming off an adrenalin rush.

'Now what would you like to drink. You can have anything, it's nearly lunchtime. Would you like a glass of wine?'

Ian thought this was a little unusual. He looked at his watch; it was nearly one o'clock.

'I just need some general advice to start with. Would

you prefer to do this over lunch? Perhaps we could have a more relaxed chat?'

'Oh, that is a good idea,' she said. 'I have just finished a major court case and been interviewed on the court steps for the one o'clock news. I only just made it here in time and I could do with a drink.'

'Lead the way!' Ian said cheerfully as he stood up. 'You choose the restaurant and I'll pay.'

'Absolutely not! You are my guest. Albrecht Berger will pay,' she insisted. 'Follow me.'

They walked a short distance from the offices to a formal restaurant with white table cloths and silver cutlery. Ingrid spoke German to the maître d' and they were sat at a prominent table in the centre of the dining room.

'Now you choose the wine,' Ingrid said. 'Order whatever you like.'

She was excited and Ian's mind was racing. He didn't often drink at lunchtime so would prefer to order just a glass of wine but if Ingrid had just won her case, perhaps champagne was more appropriate. Ian enunciated what he was thinking.

'Would you like champagne? To celebrate your victory?'

'Yes, we can have champagne but I can't drink half a bottle; I have to work later.'

'And I'm flying back to Manchester. How about a glass of white?'

'Perfect; you choose,' she said, handing Ian the wine list.

Ian scanned the offerings. All were expensive and, unusually, most were available by the glass.

'Two glasses of the Sancerre,' he said to the waitress who had come to the table, pointing to the one he had chosen.

'Certainly, Sir.'

Ingrid was starting to relax. The adrenaline was dissipating.

'Now how is it we can help you?' she asked.

The waitress returned with the wine before Ian could reply. She opened a new bottle at the table and poured some for Ian to taste. Ian raised his glass and swirling the wine, dropped his nose to the rim of the glass to smell the bouquet.

'Lovely,' Ian said without tasting it.

'Oh, what a connoisseur! You know just by the scent! I am in the hands of an expert!' Ingrid exclaimed.

Ian was slightly embarrassed by the exuberance of Ingrid's compliment but raised his glass in salute, then clinked glasses and said: 'Prost.'

'Prost,' Ingrid replied.

'I'm acting for a client who escaped through Checkpoint Charlie in 1963,' Ian started. 'She is now a successful business woman in Ireland but her father had a house just outside Berlin. Her escape was made with her boyfriend but he was captured. I was sent here to make contact with him, which I have now done and to see if there was any means of gaining title to the family property or receiving compensation for it?'

The waitress returned to the table for their order and they both chose the Dover sole. Ingrid had been considering her answer.

'A month ago, as the Wall came down, the chants were: "we are **the** people." Now they are chanting, "we are **one** people." Reunification will happen, Ian; I know it will. Yes, some people worry about the cost but the GDR is a bankrupt state and the Russians can't afford to prop it up any longer. Gorbachev doesn't have the will and Kohl will pay any price for the land. He can't argue we need Lebensraum but it is still an emotional thing. The reuniting of a people who should never have been apart.'

Ian listened attentively until the waitress brought the fish with some green beans and fondant potatoes. It was beautifully cooked and the flesh just flaked off the bone.

'So, what are you saying?' he asked.

'I'm saying wait for reunification. That will be the time to make a claim and we will be happy to represent your client when the time comes.'

'I see,' Ian said nodding. 'Thank you, that sounds like good advice.'

It may have been the wine and the fact that they were both relaxing or just two professionals discussing a common interest but Ian said: 'I suppose a lot of secrets will come out - now that the Wall is down.'

'I have no doubt about it, Ian. We are going to have a lot of work to do.'

'My client's former boyfriend is investigating a secret,' Ian continued. 'His father worked for the Vatican Bank after the War and discovered something untoward. Former Nazis smuggled abroad with false identities – even to Britain. Apparently, he documented it but died before going public.' Ian started feeling a little sick as he suddenly worried he had said too much.

'Are you helping him?' Ingrid had a razor-sharp mind and she could see exactly where Ian was coming from.

'Yes,' Ian replied rather sheepishly.

'Well, my advice to you is, follow the money.'

'What do you mean?'

'The Vatican is a wealthy state and it invested heavily in Nazi Germany before the War. They have received much criticism for that but their critics have the benefit of hindsight. After the War, however, their investments were next to worthless and I believe some shady dealings went on to recover something from the wreckage. I've been involved in correcting that – litigating over patents on behalf of the true owners; that sort of thing. That's what my case was about.'

The waitress came and took away their plates and they ordered two espressos.

'I'm still not sure how to apply this to my client's boyfriend's situation?' Ian mused.

'Look, in the grand scheme of things what does it matter if you discover some seventy-year-old janitor in the UK was a former Nazi? Yes, there may be some justice in it but the real question is why? Why was he smuggled? Follow the money Ian. Follow the money and that will tell you why.'

Ian realised he was in the presence of a highly erudite woman. He didn't say the Nazi on his radar was much more significant that a janitor but the argument still held water.

As they stood up to leave, Ian kissed Ingrid on the cheek. 'You've been a big help,' he said. 'I'm looking forward to our next meeting.'

When Wolfgang Richter reported back to his boss, Peter Schulz was incandescent.

'You mean to tell me that Sutherland has been here and gone back to the UK without you even getting close to him?'

Richter wasn't intimidated. A little under six foot and in his late thirties he had spent eighteen years in the army before joining the Stasi. His hair was brown and his body was made of solid muscle. He looked stocky but he was rock hard, physically and mentally. A ruthless combatant who thought only of the job in hand. The scariest thing about him, however, was his eyes. He had dead eyes.

The Stasi had put a check on the airports but by the time Ian's arrival had been notified to HQ and his hotel traced, Ian was on his way back to the UK. There had been no warrant for his arrest simply an instruction to Richter to follow him and report back. Unfortunately for Richter, he was always a few hours behind.

Schulz paced around his office whilst Richter stood in silence trying to avoid breathing in the smoke bellowing out of his master's mouth.

'You'd better keep a close eye on Hoffmann. Sutherland has probably given the watch to him.'

'Do you want me to get it off him?'

Schulz thought for a moment. What he needed was the secret documents. If the watch contained the secret, it was no good to him unless he could work it out. On the other hand, if Hoffmann and Sutherland had resolved the puzzle, they could lead him to the prize.

'No, leave the watch with Hoffman but arrange twenty-four-hour surveillance. I want to know his every move.'

Ian was tired as he fought his way through the Harrogate rush hour traffic to the office. The constant travel was taking it out of him and he felt his absence from the office was undermining his position at Ryders. At least it's Friday, he thought. 'Friday the 15th December,' he muttered to himself wearily. 'Nearly, Christmas.'

Sarah had put a 9.00am appointment in Ian's diary for Hayden Boyes so Ian didn't even have time for a coffee before he saw the Bentley Mulsanne pull into the carpark.

Boyes got out of the car smoking and wearing a fur coat. Ian stared out of his office window in amazement. He was wearing a fur coat! Not a coat with a fur collar but a full length, brown fur coat. Ian had never seen a man in a fur coat before.

Ian trotted down the stairs and greeted Boyes in reception.

'Would you like some coffee,' Ian asked hopefully as he was desperate for one himself.

'No thanks, I've just had breakfast.'

'This way then.'

Ian took Boyes into one of the smaller interview rooms but the usual small talk was dispensed with. This was an impatient man who wanted to give his instructions and move on.

Boyes opened his briefcase and pulled out some sales particulars. He flicked them across the table at Ian as he rifled through his other papers.

'I'm selling my flat,' he said, 'and buying a house in Leathley,' which was an expensive village outside Leeds.

Ian leafed through the sales particulars. It was a smart flat and Fentons had done a good job with the photographs. It occupied the top floor of a block overlooking the Stray with a newly fitted spa and gym created in the roof space. There was a sauna, a jacuzzi, a shower and some exercise equipment.

Boyes handed over a pile of papers.

'These are the deeds I got when I bought it.'

Ian started looking through the documents.

'They're not actually the deeds. It's a report on title but still helpful.'

Boyes half stood up to go but Ian asked him to wait.

'I'll just have a quick look through whilst you're here.'

Boyes sat back down but was restless.

A professional knows what to look for and Ian, whose suspicions had been raised by the sales particulars went straight to the heart of the problem.

'Did you create the spa in the roof space?'

'Yeah. Cost me £50k.'

'There's a problem with it, I'm afraid.'

'I got planning permission if that's what you mean; and building regs.' Boyes looked through his briefcase again.

'No, that's not the issue. If you imagine the flats as a series of shoe boxes on top of each other, you have a lease of the top shoe box for 125 years. The structure, the bricks and mortar of the building, are owned by the Landlord which is a London based property company. You own the plasterboard, the lining, if you like, and everything inside it. The problem is you have created the gym and spa in the roof space. You have broken through the ceiling of the property you lease and expanded into the structure owned by the Landlord. The roof space isn't included in your lease so you have created the gym and spa in the Landlord's property.'

Boyes looked stunned.

'I've got planning permission,' he repeated.

'That's nothing to do with it. Did you seek the Landlord's permission?'

'No.'

'Well, I'm afraid we will have to go back to the Landlord and ask if we can extend the lease to include the roof space.'

'What will that cost?' Boyes asked raising his voice.

'Well, firstly there is a risk that the Landlord might not want to grant a lease of the roof space but if it will, it will be like buying another flat so it could be quite expensive. Then there's the delay. This could take a few months to sort out.'

'What?' Boyes shouted as he stood up. 'I was told you would do a quick job and you say it will take months. I could lose my purchase.'

'I'm sorry,' Ian said, 'but you've created a title problem and it's not going to be easy to resolve it. You could pull the spa out, I suppose. It might be cheaper.'

'Well, you can fuck off,' Boyes said grabbing his papers. 'I'll find myself a decent solicitor.'

Boyes stormed out of the interview room and through the front door, bypassing reception, but not without Sarah noticing the manner of his departure.

Chapter Nine

The partners' meeting was slightly earlier this month, on the 18th December, owing to the Christmas break. Ian thought he'd better try to keep Thompson sweet over the whole Hayden Boyes issue but he couldn't find him so he went into reception.

'Do you know where Mark is?' he asked Sarah.

'He's meeting a Mrs Crockett in town for a coffee but he will be back at lunch time for the partners' meeting,' came the factual reply.

'Thanks,' Ian said walking away and finding himself recollecting cowboy films from his childhood featuring Davy Crockett and his hat with the racoon's tail. Suddenly, a thought passed through his head. He went into the secretaries' room and saw Tracy's desk was empty.

'Anyone know where Tracy is?' he asked.

'She's got the day off. Christmas shopping,' Debbie replied.

'And does anyone know where Mark is?' Ian was being mischievous now but he wanted to see what they knew.

'He's seeing a Mrs Crockett,' Debbie replied.

'He sees her a lot,' muttered one of the others.

'Thank you, ladies. Most helpful,' Ian said as he smiled and left the room.

I may be putting two and two together and getting five, Ian thought to himself, but I reckon Mrs Crockett is a secret name for Tracy Davy. The secretaries had the same idea.

The Partners' meeting was even more high fuelled than normal. Thompson didn't bother with a debate over the head of agriculture but simply put forward a proposal that it should be Steve Fell. Hannah, seconded it as a "sensible solution" and murmurs of approval ran around the table. Ian could see the partners' meeting was merely a rubber-stamping job so didn't even bother to put up any resistance. Thompson took this as a sign of weakness so decided to turn the knife even though the decision to appoint Steve Fell had already been made.

'I thought you might object but given that you lose us clients rather than gain them I suppose it is hard for you to put a counter argument,' Thompson said looking at Ian. Ian ignored him and just stared back but Ronnie Roberts was woken from his day dream.

'What's that?' he said as though startled by an alarm.

'Oh, nothing. I just got him Hayden Boyes as a client, son of Ernest Boyes and heir to the BCI fortune and within ten minutes he had the client storming out of the office and telling him to fuck off,' Thompson replied.

Ian had been keeping his powder dry but saw his chance.

'I did look for you to try to explain what had happened but you were out with Mrs Davy, er Crockett, I mean.' The other partners missed the jibe but it wasn't lost on Thompson. His face coloured and he glared back at Ian. He wondered how much Ian knew.

'Anyway, moving on,' Ian said, 'I wanted to raise the issue of secretaries' salaries. I understand you have unilaterally given Tracy and Cheryl a rise?'

All the other partners looked up. Ian could tell they had no idea.

'Is that true Mark?' Hannah asked him.

'They deserve it. They work far harder than the other secretaries. They are doing fifty letters each, a day. On average, the others don't even do half that.'

'That's besides the point,' Hannah said. 'Salaries are reviewed annually and decided upon by all the partners.'

'Yes, but since we joined the Personal Injury Group, they have had a mountain of paperwork to process. They deserve the rise now.'

'That may well be the case but you can't just decide these things on your own. It's a partnership matter.'

'I don't agree with Mark's assessment anyway,' Ian interjected. 'Tracy and Cheryl might be doing more letters than our secretaries but they use standard templates for volume work. Our secretaries are talking to clients, updating agents and acting more like paralegals.'

'More like parasites, if you ask me,' Thompson

grumbled.

'Well, you've done it now, so it will have to stand or you will look foolish but don't do it again,' Hannah said closing down the discussion. 'In future you will have to follow the proper protocol.'

'Sorry,' Thompson replied feigning regret.

Ian was disappointed with that as the final outcome and with the meeting over he told Sarah he was nipping into town for a bottle of water – he needed the fresh air.

Thompson was fuming by the rebuke. He should have left things there. He had achieved all he wanted, but a bully will continue to push the boundaries until stopped, so he marched into the secretaries' room and called all of them, except Tracy, Cheryl and an elderly secretary who worked for Hannah, into one of the meeting rooms. He sat behind the desk and they all stood in front of him, like children in front of the headmaster.

'I've given Tracy and Cheryl a rise because they work harder than all of you and we run a more profitable department and I hear you've been complaining about this when you should be grateful you've got jobs. You've had it too easy for too long and you're going to have to up your game.'

One secretary called Kate was expecting a baby and she burst into tears. Debbie put her arm around her shoulder to comfort her.

'And don't try tears on me,' Thompson continued, 'they

won't work.'

Julie had heard enough.

'We don't have to take this,' she said. 'Not from you – we don't respect you,' and with that she walked out quickly followed by the others.

Thompson stood up and in a fit of rage, threw over the desk. He stormed into Ian's office but he wasn't there so he burst into reception.

'Where's Sutherland?' he shouted. His face was puce with anger.

'He's gone into town for a bottle of water,' Sarah replied.

Thompson marched out of reception and headed in the direction of town. Ian was nearly back so they met head-to-head on the pavement about thirty yards from the office.

Thompson grabbed Ian by the lapels and screamed into his face.

'You've made an enemy of me now Sutherland. You've poisoned the secretaries against me. You will be stacking shelves in Sainsbury's by the time I've finished with you.'

Ian was surprised and worried about the commotion Thompson was making in the street. People were watching.

'Not here, Mark. Come back to the office; and get off me,' Ian said pushing Thompson's hands away from his lapels.

Thomson was still screaming something but Ian sidestepped him and went back to the office. The secretaries, minus Tracy and Cheryl, were gathered in reception. Kate was still crying and Julie was still angry. They told Ian what had happened.

'Right,' Ian said. 'I'm going to see Hannah.'

Ian went into Hannah's room and told her what had happened.

'You need to go downstairs and tell the secretaries that they are valued and appreciated. Now,' Ian demanded.

Hannah agreed but at that moment Thompson appeared in her doorway. He had calmed down, a little. He started defending himself, saying something about doing all the work and not getting any support.

'You're overwrought,' Hannah said. 'I want you to take a week's holiday. Leave now,' she said firmly. Then as an afterthought she said: 'but shake hands before you go.'

Thompson looked sheepish and held out his hand to Ian. Ian automatically responded and Thompson gave him a weak handshake. 'Sorry,' he said and walked away.

'That's it!' Ian remonstrated. 'That's it! He attacks me in the street and you give him a week's holiday?'

'That's it for now,' Hannah replied. 'Now let's have a word with these secretaries.'

They went down to see the secretaries and Hannah just repeated what Ian had suggested.

'You're all valued and appreciated,' she kept reassuring them whilst one called Janet said Thompson was a "bastard" and Kate continued breaking into tears.

'I want an emergency partners' meeting now,' Ian said in a way that indicated it was a demand not a request and as the other partners had started coming out of their offices and were hanging around the corridor, peering through the doorway, Hannah agreed.

In the boardroom, Ian explained what had happened but he was cognisant of the fact that Steve Fell was with them and would repeat everything to Thompson.

'He has a divisive style of management,' Ian said 'and unless we give all the secretaries the same rise, we will have a war on our hands.'

It was agreed that all the secretaries should be given the same rise as Tracy and Cheryl and Hannah would tell them today but no one suggested any sanctions on Thompson. They did not approve of his behaviour but no one, apart from Ian, was prepared to challenge him. The power of money was strong.

That evening Ian sank into the Jag and drove home without the radio on, reflecting on the day. In this latest debacle with Thompson he had won the day or, at least, fended him off, but if you read the runes, it was clear the partnership was doomed.

Ian rushed into the kitchen and told Sophie all about it but her reaction was not quite what he had been expecting. Ian had spent too much time away from home, too much time out of the office and too much time thinking about Theo and Angela rather than his own relationship with

Sophie. She had left her home in Germany and got a job in Durham to be with Ian but he wouldn't think beyond the next day. She wanted to make a home and she felt he was more concerned about making a reputation. Mulling over things alone she had become more and more frustrated.

'I'm going home for Christmas,' she said at last.

'Oh,' Ian replied taken by surprise. 'Okay, I'll come with you.'

'No, you need to stay here to look after Sky.'

'We can put her in kennels.'

'No, I need some space. I'm fed up with the dark, damp weather, I'm fed up with all your partnership problems and I'm fed up with you.' Her voice trailed off with the last part of the sentence.

'I see,' Ian said quietly. 'Well, if you don't mind, I'm going for a run.'

Sophie was longing for him to fight back. To say he would sort out the problems. To say she was more important than everything else. To say he loved her. But Ian was too proud for that. She had insulted him and he needed time to process the situation.

Ian put on his tracksuit and, hanging a dog whistle around his neck, he set off with Sky. He had trained her that two short blasts on the whistle meant "come" and one long blast meant "stop." She was off the lead and he was going to run through the deer park so he hoped she wouldn't chase anything and especially not a deer but Ian didn't want to run with her on the lead and he wasn't in a mood to compromise.

A sensible person would consider it too dark to run off road but Ian wasn't feeling sensible; he was feeling stubborn. The driveway up to St Mary's church was wet and the surface water glistened in the moonlight. It was cold. Ian didn't blame Sophie for her comments about the weather; it was miserable. Ian turned left, downhill towards the lake but kept on the tarmac until he reached the wooden footbridge at the bottom of the lake. He crossed over, Sky following just behind him and then, rather than taking the route of the seven bridges, Ian ran up a muddy track towards a large expanse of open land. As he approached a kissing gate he slipped and fell on his knee. He must have surprised an owl because one spookily took off above his head and flew away from him. Back on his feet, Ian continued the gentle climb up the stony track across the open aspect of land, the sky providing just enough light for him to see. Half way up the hill the track came to an end and now his trainers squelched in the soft ground letting in water and soaking his feet.

He was prepared to admit he had been preoccupied. Theo had a mystery and he wanted to solve it. He wasn't sure about Angela and there was definitely something dodgy about her husband. Did she know what he was up to? And then there was Thompson. The girls were right. He was a bastard. But Ryders was still the best firm in

Harrogate and partners didn't usually change firms. Where else could he go? I'd rather do something completely different, he thought.

Tempest was a miserable old git but he wasn't as bad as Hayden Boyes. That had to be a set up. Ian had taken an instant dislike to him (why waste time?) and he reckoned Thompson knew he would, but Thompson couldn't have known about the problems with the flat. Anyway, he was glad to be rid of him. Ian preferred choosing his own clients. Hannah had been too weak though. She had stood up to Thompson a little, but it was more a matter of containment than actually dealing with the problem. She just didn't know what direction to take. At least the secretaries were on his side. He was their hero. So how could Sophie say she was fed up with him? He was doing his best. Doing what was right. That was unfair. She needed to support him more. It would be all right in the end. He would sort it out. She should trust him to do so. He never lost. Never gave in. He was determined to win.

He was running downhill now. Back on a stony track towards the village; a gentle sweat on his brow. Sky had stayed close. Perhaps she sensed it was a tense situation. Ian thought about John Field and Manfred Fuchs. That was a similar situation. A mysterious death. A dark secret. I wonder what Simon Black would make of all this, Ian thought.

He got back to the cottage. Sophie had gone to bed.

In Marylebone, Simon Black was working late. He needed a big win to keep his job and triumph over Rebecca Topping but the MI6 files that he could access revealed nothing and he doubted Schulz would produce the goods. He wanted the information because that would give him leverage. Power over others – the thing he most enjoyed. He drew an upright oblong on a sheet of paper, like a door. Behind that door was a secret, and Ian Sutherland was the key.

Chapter Ten

Christmas is meant to be a happy time of year but for many people it is a difficult time because the festivities highlight any shortcomings in one's relationships and the feeling that you should be happy just makes matters worse.

Ian spent Christmas Day with his family and Boxing Day taking Sky a long walk but for the rest of the holiday he was in the office, catching up on paperwork and, if he was honest about it, he was glad to be there.

The one bright note was a call from Theo who agreed a date for their trip to Rome on Wednesday 17th January which Ian, likewise, agreed with Angela before confirming. They would be arriving from three different locations but Angela had agreed with Ian's choice of hotel, the d'Inghilterra, near the Spanish Steps. Theo had made his own arrangements.

Wolfgang Richter had been alerted to Theo's flight information by the travel agent in Berlin and reported back to Schulz. Schulz was slumped in his chair, smoking as he tried to pass away the time anxiously waiting for Hoffmann and Sutherland to make their next move. The appearance of Richter made him sit upright with anticipation.

'Good. Book us a flight on the same day. Not the same flight because Hoffmann will recognise me. Make it an earlier one, and find out where he is staying.'

Richter nodded and left the room. Schulz telephoned Black. The situation in East Berlin was becoming chaotic. The calls for reunification were growing stronger and there was no support for the existing regime coming from Moscow. The Stasi were destroying their records as surreptitiously as they could but with files on six million people it was no easy task and Schulz was eager to defect before the recriminations started.

'Hoffmann has arranged a visit to Rome on the 17th January,' Schulz said. 'We will let him collect the information and then get it off him and bring it to you.' Schulz did not mention Ian because he had assumed Theo had the watch.

'I will meet you there,' Black replied wanting to keep the negotiations a secret from his colleagues for as long as possible. However, there was no way he was going to rely on Schulz. That would be far too simple. Black liked to complicate things. See how the different scenarios played out. Besides if he could bypass Schulz and save the taxpayer a bit of money, it was a job well done. He picked up the telephone and rang Monsignor Demarco Marchetti.

'Theo Hoffmann is coming to Rome and I think Ian Sutherland will be with him, as he collected the watch from Dublin. Presumably, he will have the watch with him, they will meet up in Rome and both collect the information. I can let you know when Sutherland arrives on the understanding that we share the information. I don't want anything that embarrasses the Vatican but I do want to see anything of interest to British intelligence.' Schulz had not mentioned Ian's earlier visit to Berlin so Black assumed, correctly as it happened, that Ian still had the watch.

'Agreed, and it should be easier to get the watch off Sutherland than from a Lutheran priest,' Marchetti replied, already mulling over a plot in his mind.

'I wouldn't bank on it,' Black said knowingly. 'Anyway, do we want the watch? Shouldn't we wait until they collect the information?'

'No. We must intercept them before the information gets into the wrong hands.'

'What if we can't decipher the code?'

'Then we leave it where it is. This dog has been sleeping for 40 years. We don't have to wake it.'

'I see,' Black said somewhat perturbed. He needed the information to save his career and did not want to let sleeping dogs lie. He now realised that his interests were more aligned with Schulz than the Roman Catholic Church but thought it was as well to keep both hares running.

Marchetti put down the telephone and addressed his envoy, Father Jacob, in his usual peremptory manner.

'Get me a driver,' he said to the little old man.

Father Jacob was both little, being just over five feet tall and old, in so far as he was in his early seventies. His frame was also slightly hunched and his body frail, but he had a sharp mind and he was taking a particular interest in his master's current affairs. He hailed a driver and Marchetti got in the back of a black Range Rover that was seven years old with less than 14,000 miles on the clock.

'Take me to the Ferrari dealership,' he said to the driver's surprise.

Monsignor Demarco Marchetti didn't know the details of Werner Hoffmann's objections all those years ago, other than it was something to do with the Church's assistance to Ukrainian refugees. He sighed at the prospect of what he was about to arrange. Always clearing up after other people's mess he thought, although, he did believe that for the last hundred years the Roman Catholic Church had been unlucky.

First the Church lost its lands and primary source of wealth with the rise of Italian nationalism. Then the break-up of the Austro-Hungarian empire and the spread of Bolshevism weakened the Catholic stronghold in Central Europe. People like Hoffmann just didn't get it. It was not the Nazis the Church feared. It was the Communists.

Many of those fleeing from countries such as the Ukraine at the end of the War were Catholics. Didn't the Church have a responsibility towards them? These were people who had supported Germany during the War and they were fleeing for their lives. If the Russians caught up with them they would be slaughtered. Western Intelligence knew what the Church was doing and condoned it as they too considered the Communists the enemy and the refugees a useful source of intelligence about what was going on behind the Iron Curtain. Okay, a few undesirables may have slipped through the net but this was an unavoidable outcome of the broader policy.

On arrival, Marchetti walked through the large glass doors of the showroom barely giving the portfolio of supercars a second glance. He went to the back of the showroom where there was a small office partitioned off by more glass. He could see Rocco Morelli sat behind a small desk and he knocked on the door and walked straight in without waiting for an answer.

Morelli lifted his head in surprise and looked worried. He stood up awkwardly. He was tall and slim with brown hair and a fringe. It was a schoolboy's haircut that he had never bothered to change. He smiled broadly revealing a full set of slightly overcrowded and discoloured teeth. Marchetti held out his hand and Morelli kissed the ring.

'I haven't seen you in church for a while, Rocco,' Marchetti said reprehensively.

Morelli gave an awkward grin and shrugged his shoulders. 'What can I say, I've been busy.'

'That's what your wife tells me!' Marchetti retorted, and then more softly he continued: 'She's a good woman and I like it when she brings your daughters.' Morelli looked embarrassed.

'She tells me you have affairs?'

'I thought confessions were confidential?' Morelli replied, somewhat indignantly.

'I'm not telling you anything you don't already know and anyway, it's not her confession.' Morelli had no answer to that.

'She has turned a blind eye in the past but now you seem to have concentrated your affections on one particularly attractive mistress?'

'She's an attractive woman but I'm still a family man,' Morelli replied, implying he still believed the state of marriage was inviolable.

'The choice may not be yours, Rocco. Your wife feels she cannot stay with you if you love another woman, but she is worried, that if she divorces you, the business will not survive the withdrawal of capital.'

'She's threatened divorce before but she will never go through with it,' Morelli said defensively.

Marchetti smiled and took off his glasses. Wearily, he drew his thumb and index finger down the centre of his forehead and nose and then let his fingers separate as they tracked the sides of his mouth and re-joined at the bottom of his chin. He put his glasses back on and looked up at Morelli.

'It's that confidence that makes her think you take her

for granted and for the church, it's difficult. Traditionally, we have always been against divorce but views are changing. I'm struggling how to counsel her.'

Morelli suddenly sensed that Marchetti was brokering a deal.

'What do you want of me?' he asked.

'There's a young lawyer coming to town by the name of Ian Sutherland – English. He will have a large pocket watch with him which we need. I won't bore you with why. I thought, perhaps, one of your lady friends could befriend him and relieve it from his person. We don't want any violence,' he emphasized, 'and this seems an altogether more agreeable solution.'

'That's it?' Morelli questioned.

'Yes.'

'And I assume that if I am successful in acquiring the watch the church will stick to its traditional teaching?'

'Of course.'

Morelli stood up again, indicating the deal was done and Marchetti did likewise.

'I will let you know when Sutherland arrives,' Marchetti said.

'No problem,' Morelli replied, laughing as he spoke. 'I thought you were going to ask for a Ferrari.'

It was four weeks since Ian had last seen Tempest Huber and he had put him to the back of his mind, so he was taken by surprise when Sarah said he had left a message asking for a new Will.

'When did he ring?' Ian asked.

'Just now.'

'Did he say anything else?'

'No, he just said would I ask you to go and see him about a new Will.'

'Well, this will be the fourth Will I've made for him in less than two months!' Ian complained.

If he was looking for sympathy he wasn't going to get it from Sarah who always took the client's side, so reluctantly he gave in.

'Okay, can you ring him back and say I will call in on my way home at about 4.30pm?

The farmstead looked eerie in the late afternoon gloom and barren with all the hen huts burnt; a sort of smouldering wasteland with the yellow glow of a kitchen light acting as a beacon of hope. Formerly, it had looked a mess, but it was teeming with life. Now it had the smell of death.

Ian made his way to the back door which was slightly ajar and called out.

'Hello, Mr Huber. How are you?'

'Surviving. Come on in.'

Tempest was sat in his usual chair but his skin looked grey and he was even more unkempt.

'I understand you want to change your Will again?' Ian bit his lip when he said "again" but he couldn't help it.

'Yes, I just want to leave everything to my niece, Mary

James.'

'Oh, why's that?' Ian queried.

'Since I came home my son has brought me a meal every night cooked by his wife. I said, "that's very good of her you must let me give her something for her trouble," and he said, "I'll ask her." Next day he came round with a meal and said, "she thought about £100!" That's £5 a day! I pulled open my kitchen drawer,' at this point Tempest did so to reveal a rolled wad of notes with a rubber band around them, 'stripped off some notes and said, "I never want to see you again." And I haven't.'

'Gosh, well erm, it may have cost about £5 to make the meal and maybe she thought you would feel better if you were paying for it,' Ian said, trying to find grounds for reconciliation.

'It won't have cost anything like that. I know all about food. I grew up on a farm. No, they thought I was made of money, more like. They've just got their eye on the main chance. Well, they can forget it.'

'I see,' Ian said a little embarrassed. It was obvious that Tempest's mind was made up.

'Are you absolutely sure you want to leave everything to your niece?'

'Yes. She comes round every day and says, "what do you need?" I say, "some toothpaste," and the next day she brings it and says, "that's 37p," and that's how I like it.'

'Okay, however, there are a couple of things I should

mention. Your son could make a claim against your estate. He is certainly within the category of people who can make a claim but as he is of full age and not in any way being maintained by you, it may not be a very strong claim. The second issue is that you will only have one executor and for practical reasons it is better to have two. It is also more difficult to sell land if you only have one.'

'Well, you can be the second executor and if he makes a claim, you can fight it. I don't want him to have another penny.'

'All right,' Ian said. 'I will get this drawn up and come back as soon as I can.'

Within twenty-four hours Ian was back with the new Will accompanied by Ed Tucker and Debbie as, being an executor, Ian was unable to act as a witness.

At least, with all the livestock gone the smell wasn't quite as overwhelming but Ian was still shocked on entering the kitchen. Tempest was sat in his usual chair but the side of his head was badly bruised and coloured purple. So were his hands.

'I've brought your new Will, Mr Huber,' Ian said, 'and Debbie and Ed have come with me to act as witnesses.'

Tempest stretched out his arm to take the Will. It was also bruised and purple.

'Good because I might not be around much longer,' he said in that melodramatic way which attaches itself to the elderly. 'I was beaten up last night.'

'What?' Ian exclaimed as all three of them looked on with shock.

'Two youths broke in and tied me to the chair and stole my money. I tried to fight them off but they overpowered me. The chair fell over sideways as I tried to escape and I banged my head on the hearth.'

'Have you called the police?' Ian asked.

'No, I don't want any trouble. They'll have been sent round by my son. He was the only one who knew where my money was and they went straight for it. Well, he can have it, but he won't get any more.'

Ian raised his eyebrows in disbelief but Tempest was not a man to be argued with. He was stubborn and obstinate, as his self-discharge from hospital had revealed, so Ian got the Will signed and left checking that Tempest would be all right until Mary came round the next morning.

There was no next morning for Tempest. When Mary pushed open the kitchen door, she saw Tempest lying on the floor. She ran over to him and put her hand on his neck to check his pulse but it was horribly cold. She grabbed his hand but it was cold and hard. Lifeless, like a stone. She called 999 and within minutes there was an ambulance on site and a doctor who had driven himself. He said Tempest had passed away in the night.

Ian was shocked when he heard the news because Tempest must have died within a few hours of signing his Will. He felt a bit bad about complaining, however, as an executor, he had things to do. It was less than a week until Ian was scheduled to go to Rome so he arranged to meet Mary at the house the next day, Friday, to explain the formalities and he took Debbie with him as a safeguard. When going through a deceased person's belongings it was protocol to have a witness to the events.

Mary led them from the kitchen to the dining room. It was packed with antique furniture with just enough room to squeeze through to the staircase. The furniture looked expensive; wardrobes and chests of drawers in the Dutch marquetry style.

'This is a bit of a surprise,' Ian said, as he had never been beyond the kitchen before.

'He worked at Tennants Auctioneers as a part-time porter after he retired and bought things that didn't attract much interest,' Mary replied.

'Oh, that's a great business,' Ian said. 'I have a lot of respect for the Tennant family.'

They pressed through to the staircase and Mary cracked open the sitting room door revealing a room equally crammed with antique furniture. Ian took a peek through the doorway but noticing the strong, musky smell, he didn't bother going in.

'Where did he work before Tennants?' Ian asked to make conversation as they made their way upstairs.

'BCI. It's a chemical company in Leeds run by a family friend, Ernest Boyes. They came over together from Italy after the War.'

Ian stopped in his tracks on the little square landing at the top of the stairs.

'Are you saying Tempest was Italian?'

'No, he was Ukrainian. He was a prisoner of war in Rimini and he came to the UK in 1947 with my mother. Ernest Boyes gave him a job because they had served in the army together.'

Before Ian could react, Mary opened the door into one of the bedrooms.

'This was my mother's room. She moved in with him after my father died and then she died about five years ago. He hasn't touched it since and he didn't want me going through her things either. They were very close.'

Ian glanced around and noticed a dressing table with a Liberty vanity set and other Art Nouveau novelties scattered about the room. Cobwebs hung from the corners of the ceiling.

Mary shut the door and wafted her way past the bathroom and a spare room to Tempest's bedroom. It was filthy with dust and grime. It probably hadn't seen a vacuum for five years.

'He kept everything important in there,' Mary said pointing to a black metal deeds box. The key was in it.

'Okay, I suppose we'd better have a look,' Ian said, still mulling over Mary's words. 'Debbie, can you keep a note of what I find and what we take away with us?'

'Yes,' Debbie replied, pulling a notepad out of a slim file.

Ian opened the lid and peered inside. On the top lay several building society passbooks with a rubber band around them. Ian opened each one and carried out a mental calculation. The savings amounted to about £600,000. Much more than he had expected.

'We'll keep these,' he said to Mary. 'I'll write to each of the building societies, send them a copy of the death certificate and get an exact balance as at the date of death. We will need it for inheritance tax purposes.'

'Will we have to pay inheritance tax?' Mary asked.

'Looks like it,' Ian replied.

He then pulled out an A4 sized, brown folder made of card and tied together with red ribbon. It contained the deeds to the smallholding and Ian was quickly able to confirm that the land was purchased in the name of Tempest Huber in 1948.

'I still think *Tempest* is an unusual Christian name,' Ian said.

'It was just a nickname,' Mary explained, 'because he had a terrible temper but when he left Italy he had to change his name so Ernest suggested *Huber* because it means *farmer* and he kept his nickname although *Storm* would be a more accurate translation.'

Ian continued digging and found a birth certificate, an expired passport and a driving licence, all in the name of

Tempest Huber.

'The estate looks fairly straightforward,' he said as he pulled out another brown envelope, A4 in length but only half the width.

Ian peered inside. There was a folded newspaper cutting from Das Reich and something solid in the bottom of the envelope. Ian turned it upside down and a badge fell out. It was in the shape of a shield with dark yellow edging and a mid-blue background. A standing heraldic yellow lion filled the space with two crowns at the top of the shield and one at the bottom. At first, Ian thought there was some Royal connection but on the back was inscribed: "14. Waffen-Grenadier-Division der SS."

'What's this?' Ian asked.

'He was in the Galician SS,' Mary replied. 'They weren't like the German SS,' she added quickly. 'It was mainly made up of volunteers from Ukraine who wanted independence from Russia. They were freedom fighters really and uncle said they were only used to fight the Bolsheviks. Ernest Boyes was his commanding officer.'

'So, is Ernest Boyes Ukrainian?' Ian asked.

'No, he's Austrian. The officers were usually of the Aryan race.'

Ian thought that was an unusual turn of phrase. He opened up the newspaper cutting. It was a photograph of several soldiers with names inscribed underneath.

'Is this your uncle?' Ian asked, pointing at one of the

soldiers that looked familiar.

'Yes, that's him and that's Ernest.'

Ian looked at the name underneath.

'Hadeon Kolesnik?'

'Yes, that was uncle's name before he changed his identity. Ernest named his son after him because he said he saved his life.'

'So, Ernest Boyes was called Ernst Junger?' Ian continued, trying to process the rapid flow of information.

'Yes, he wouldn't change his first name because he was a Baron and they were all called Ernst. Uncle became his sort of batman.'

'So, an Austrian Baron becomes an officer in the Galician SS, meets your uncle and they end up in an Italian prisoner of war camp and then emigrate to Britain. Is that what you're telling me?'

'Yes.'

'So, if they were prisoners of war, how come your mother came over with them?' Ian asked genuinely puzzled by the story.

Mary buried her face in her hands and burst into tears.

'Oh, I can't bear the lies any longer,' she said, squinting through her fingers. 'I'm not his niece; I'm his daughter.'

Chapter Eleven

Debbie had missed the details because she had gone to get Mary a glass of water when she burst into tears.

'So, what did she say?' Debbie asked as they drove back to the office in the E-Type.

Ian raised his eyebrows.

'Where do I start?' he exclaimed. 'Mary said that when Tempest came to England, he had a fling with a well-known Ripon floozy who had a son – Bobbie Baxter. Tempest wasn't sure if he was the father and had nothing more to do with her or the baby. Then he met Mary's mother and they fell in love but she was already married to an older, disabled man and she already had a son, Richard. Tempest and Mary's mother struck up a relationship and, not surprisingly, along came Mary. Tempest was a regular visitor to their family home and assumed the role of an uncle. Then when her mother's husband died, her mother moved in with Tempest, purporting to the World that they were brother and sister.'

'Gosh,' Debbie said. 'You just never know what goes on behind closed doors.'

Reading files intently in the privacy of his office,

Monsignor Demarco was interrupted by Father Jacob when he knocked on one of the huge doors and asked for some time off to take a holiday. Demarco thought nothing of it. Given his age, Father Jacob shouldn't be working at all, really, but it was not unusual to forego retirement in the Vatican. It was a way of life and Father Jacob had lived there since the War.

Demarco also knew Father Jacob was Ukrainian and that his name was, actually, Yakiv. What he did not know was anything about his background. Frankly, he wasn't interested, but when Father Jacob had said he was taking his holiday in England, Demarco did think it unusual. However, it was none of his business so he didn't ask any questions.

England would not have been Father Jacob's first choice for a holiday either but then this wasn't a holiday. It was a mission. In fact, it was a continuation of a mission he started long ago in his motherland.

Born in 1916, he was too young to remember Galicia being incorporated into Poland, at the end of the First World War, despite its majority Ukrainian population. He did, however, remember it being annexed by the Soviets in 1939 when Poland was divided between the Soviet Union and Germany.

He had wanted to fight for his country's independence, and the occupation by Germany and the formation of the Galician SS in 1943 seemed the perfect opportunity to do so, but he was too small. Standing at just over five feet tall, he failed to reach the minimum height requirements. However, he was clearly intelligent and his local bishop, Bishop Bucko, who shared the same political beliefs, had recommended a career in the church as a clever solution. The Ukrainian Catholic Church had demanded the presence of chaplains in the newly formed SS division and so his desire to serve his country was secured through this rather unorthodox route.

Regrettably, for Father Jacob, the Galician SS barely survived two years before surrendering to the British in May 1945, but the bonds he formed with his comrades were sealed with blood and were to last a lifetime. He shuddered as he suppressed some of the memories.

He was interned in the British camp at Rimini as a prisoner of war but, once again, Bishop Bucko came to the rescue. Bucko appealed to Pope Pius XII who was known to be pro German, to intervene on behalf of the Galician SS, saying they were good Catholics and fervent anti-Communists. The Pope agreed and made representations to the Allies that as former citizens of Poland, they should not be deported to the Soviet Union. This gave the British a dilemma. They couldn't keep them locked up forever so they fell back on the usual Great British compromise. The British changed their status from prisoners of war to enemy personnel thus enabling thousands of former soldiers to immigrate to the United Kingdom and Canada without even the minimal screening normally required. The names of those entering the United Kingdom via this route were recorded in the so called "Rimini List," but this list had never been made public.

Father Jacob, being a chaplain, had been treated differently. For two years, whilst interned in the Rimini camp he had assisted the Vatican Information Service and the International Red Cross with the processing of the inmates. He helped his comrades reconstruct their identities; often false identities washed clean of their sins and validated by false identity cards and new passports procured from the Red Cross under false pretences. He had no qualms with what he was doing. War was brutal and he was being true to his beliefs.

Following this service, in 1947, he was offered a staff position with the VIS and moved to Rome. He knew too much. He knew the inside story and he suspected that, as the Vatican's banker, Werner Hoffman had known much of it as well. If Hoffman had hidden information in a safe deposit box, he could have his own version of the Rimini List showing the fugitives' true and false identities. It was this concern that now brought him to the paint works at the Cross Green Industrial Estate in Leeds to meet with one of the most notorious names from the list.

An attractive secretary guided Father Jacob through an ugly building to an office on a mezzanine floor. It was functionally furnished with views of the carpark to the rear and a window at the front overlooking the shop floor. It was workmanlike, designed for someone wanting to micro-manage rather than impress. Still Ernest Boyes was dressed in a smart suit and smiled when he stood up to greet the church's envoy.

Father Jacob recognised Boyes immediately. They knew each other but not well. For a couple of years, during the War, they shared the same journey although some distance apart but, nevertheless, Ernst Junger was a man Father Jacob revered. Many in Galicia viewed him as a leader who had taken on their enemies and almost won, so Father Jacob had been a willing participant in the organisation of his escape to Britain in 1947.

They were of a similar age but Boyes still has his Nordic good looks. His blonde hair had gone grey but he was tall and slim and he emanated power.

'Do sit down,' Boyes said indicating a chair at the front of his desk. 'Would you like a drink?'

'No thank you. I have a very delicate stomach so I have to be careful, especially when I am away from home.' Father Jacob nearly continued by saying his insides had never recovered from eating grass as the Galician SS fought or retreated its way through Slovakia, depending on how you looked at it. However, he decided there was no need to bring up unpleasant memories.

'So, what brings you to England Yakiv? It's been a long time.'

Father Jacob smiled. It had been a long time since anyone had used the Ukrainian version of his name and perhaps Boyes did so to acknowledge their shared past.

'It has been a long time,' Father Jacob replied, in a heavily accented English. 'Over 40 years! Life has treated you well?'

'Life has been kind to me,' Boyes replied sweeping his right arm in a large semi-circle to indicate the extent of his empire. 'I am the majority owner in BCI which is the largest privately owned paint business in the UK.'

Father Jacob nodded as he looked around although all he could see was the factory floor and some fancy cars in the carpark.

'Family?' he asked.

'A wife and a son, Hayden.' Boyes paused momentarily. 'I named him after Kolesnik! He exclaimed. 'You remember him?'

Father Jacob nodded but he only knew him as Boyes's sidekick.

'He just passed away actually,' Boyes continued as he looked down at the floor. His daughter rang me a couple of days ago.'

'I'm sorry,' Father Jacob replied.

'I owe my life to him. When the War ended, we went into hiding in the Austrian Alps for over a year and he kept me alive with his foraging. We begged milk off the farmers and broke into mountain huts where shepherds often left supplies but, other than that, we lived off the land.'

'It must have been difficult,' Father Jacob said, nodding sympathetically.

'Feast or famine. Sometimes, we would bag a chamois and gorge ourselves before burying the remaining carcass in the snow. But mainly it was nettle soup or dandelion salad. Kolesnik knew what was safe to eat. I had no idea.'

'I'm surprised the Americans didn't find you. That area was crawling with them – searching for refugees following the ratline.'

'We stayed above two thousand feet. The Americans were too lazy to climb above the treeline.'

'So, how did you end up in Rimini?' Father Jacob asked, trying to fill in the gaps between the end of the War and Boyes arrival at Rimini.

'We were making our way to Rome, like everyone else, with a view to emigrating to Argentina but I only had an identity card that I had taken from a dead soldier. I had changed the photograph but to get to Argentina I needed a passport, visa, and preferably, a birth certificate. These things cost money so as we crossed the border into Italy, we found accommodation in Merano and work at an automotive paint factory in Bolzano. I liked it there. I posed as Tyrolean, the locals spoke German and there was a shortage of workers as all the Jews had been deported. After a year, I was running the place and I was just starting to think I could start a new life in Italy, when some Jew boy recognised me.'

'That's what I wanted to talk to you about. I have some information for you from the VIS,' Father Jacob said, to give his warning more authority. 'You will understand that I do not know all the details and can only tell you what I know.'

Boyes knew that Father Jacob was setting out the ground rules. He also knew that, just like after the War, he was expected to accept whatever was offered.

'I understand,' Boyes replied.

'The VIS is fearful that your cover may be blown and suggests you spend some time abroad. I am asked to assure you that we have the matter in hand but in case anything goes wrong you need to be vigilant.'

Boyes was listening carefully, analysing every word that was said.

'What would cause my cover to be blown after all this time?'

'The whistle blower, Werner Hoffman, who nearly blew your cover in 1947, had a son called Theo. It appears that before he died, he sequestrated all the sensitive information in a safe deposit box. The secret to the whereabouts of that safe deposit box is contained within a watch which Hoffman sent to his son before he died. By a quirk of fate, the watch has spent the last 30 years in Ireland but now it is being returned to the son by an English lawyer called Ian Sutherland. We understand they are meeting in Rome shortly, presumably to see what the safety deposit box contains.'

Boyes shifted uncomfortably in his seat and lent forward.

'And do you know what it contains?' he asked.

'In all probability, it will contain details of your true identity, and evidence to link that to your new identity. It may have details of the assets purchased by BCI which the Vatican would find, let's say, embarrassing and it may even have something about Huta Pieniacka.'

Boyes grimaced as Father Jacob mentioned the name of the village.

'They were guerrillas. They killed my men,' he replied defensively.

'They were Poles,' Father Jacob shrugged dismissively. 'Poles, Russians and Jews.'

Boyes sat back in his chair and sighed.

'Can you give me a date by which time I should be on holiday?'

'The 17th January.'

Boyes shuffled restlessly. That didn't give him long.

'Can you tell me anything else?'

'No, but I will let you know when the danger has passed.'

Boyes stood up and held out his right hand. Father Jacob clasped it tightly and Boyes brought down his left hand on top and patted the back of Father Jacob's hand.

'Please pass on my thanks to the VIS and inform them that from tomorrow I shall be on my yacht in the Mediterranean. I shall be just off the coast of Rome, but still in international waters.'

Chapter Twelve

The Hotel D'Inghilterra provided an excellent location close to the Spanish Steps where Ian had agreed to meet Theo at 6pm.

The flight from Manchester was uneventful and the hotel was comfortable although somewhat formal. Ian's room had dark red wallpaper and mahogany furniture with shutters on the windows. There was a courtly feel about the place. Ian didn't pay too much attention however as he was there on business so he unpacked and headed for the famous rendezvous point.

The sun had already set, but the area was buzzing with life as the afternoon changed to evening and people either raced home or met up to enjoy a night out together.

Ian stood facing the steps, soaking in the atmosphere and within a couple of minutes he saw Theo appear at the top, trotting down a couple of steps at a time.

'You made it then?' Theo said, giving Ian a one-armed hug. Ian wasn't used to such a demonstrative expression of male affection but responded in kind, patting Theo on the back.

'Yes, no problem. Everything went like clockwork,'

Ian said pulling the watch out of his pocket and waving it in front of Theo.

'Excellent, well let's go, shall we? We'll have to get a taxi. The villa is a 20-minute drive out of town.'

It took almost an hour as Theo hadn't allowed for rush hour and the fact that traffic had increased since his father's time.

They got the taxi to drop them outside a trattoria and then walked to the Villa Stella Rossa which was a few hundred yards up the main road.

The driveway was, perhaps 50 yards long and bounded on either side by a mature shrubbery so it was like walking down a wooded corridor until the canopy opened up and the driveway made a circle around a grassed area with a large granite rock in its centre. On top of the rock was a framed piece of stained glass depicting an angel with its hands and face raised towards heaven. Ian stared at it, almost in disbelief. Suddenly, their adventure was becoming very real.

'You ought to see it first thing in the morning,' Theo said. 'It looks glorious with the sunlight shining through it.'

Ian didn't answer as he was checking out the house. Built in the classical style, it had a front porch with two pillars at either side topped with a pediment. There was a light shining down from the pediment but no other lights could be seen from the front of the house.

'It doesn't look like anyone is in,' Ian said looking

round nervously. 'I think we'll just have to risk it.'

Theo pulled a small canvas cloth from his jacket pocket which he had wrapped around a monkey wrench and a screw driver.

'Hopefully, one of these will work,' he said.

The stained-glass frame was affixed to a dark metal base and this was attached to a square of polished granite which was, itself, bolted on to the lump of granite rock. The only thing that could easily be removed was the four-bolt connection between the metal base and the polished granite.

Theo set the monkey wrench to the right size and attempted to loosen the first bolt. The first turn was difficult as years of weathering had almost sealed the bolt to the base but as soon as it loosened it came out quite quickly. Likewise, with the second but the third bolt wouldn't shift and the monkey wrench shaved off two of the edges as it slipped under the pressure of the twist.

'Careful or there will be nothing left to grip,' Ian said, as his eyes scanned the boundaries in case anyone was approaching.

Theo shifted the monkey wrench to the adjacent grip point and tried again, this time just increasing the pressure gradually. Luckily, the bolt yielded, and the fourth bolt came away more easily, perhaps loosened by the agitation of the base beneath it.

Ian gently lifted the sculpture vertically. There was

nothing to see on the polished granite and no space to hide anything but as Ian lifted, Theo bent at the waist and peered upwards at the metal base.

'Wait! I can see something,' he shouted excitedly. 'There's something taped to the bottom.'

Ian held the sculpture high, his arms straining under the weight, as Theo started to pull away the black plastic tape.

'It's a keyring, with two keys,' Theo said, as he inspected his find.

Ian was facing the driveway; Theo had his back towards it. Suddenly, it was flooded by light.

'Oh my God, there's a car coming! Quick we've got to go,' Ian said lowering the angel to the ground.

'It's too late. They'll see us,' Theo replied with panic in his voice.

'It doesn't matter. Just run.'

Ian shot down the drive just as a dark grey Fiat saloon approached. Theo was struggling to keep up and Ian could hear his heavy breathing so as he passed the car he banged on the roof shouting like a hooligan. They made it to the main road and kept running.

'What did you do that for?' Theo asked, as he bent double, gasping for breath.

'To frighten them, so they wouldn't chase us,' Ian replied.

They slowed to a jogging pace and made it back to the trattoria. They tried to look normal, but Theo was sweating and red-faced and even Ian was breathing deeply, probably as a result of the adrenalin pumping through his veins. They ordered a drink and asked the owner to ring for a taxi but he kept watching them suspiciously so they sat at the far end of the bar whilst they waited.

Ian pulled the keys out of his pocket attached to a small rectangular keyring which was more like a dog-tag. Engraved on the back was the name of a bank: Banca Monte dei Paschi di Siena and the address in Via del Corso near Trajan's column. There was also a four-digit number, 1135.

Theo slid the keyring across the table to Ian.

'What do you think the number is?' Ian asked.

'It could be the number of the safe deposit box. We'll go to the bank tomorrow, as soon as they open.'

Ian nodded. 'That's fine with me. I can't wait to see what we find.'

They made their way back to the D'Inghilterra and the concierge confirmed that Angela had arrived so Ian telephoned her and arranged to meet in the foyer at 9.00pm with Theo. Ostensibly, they were all going out for a meal together but Ian had already decided he would say "hello" and then make his excuses.

'Just time for me to get changed,' Theo said as he waved good-bye.

Ian was nervous on their behalf. They hadn't seen each other for twenty-six years. Since their separation, at Checkpoint Charlie, Angela had married and had a daughter whilst Theo had been captured by the Stasi and become a priest.

Ian exited the lift with Angela and Theo was stood there, waiting. Ian immediately felt superfluous.

'You look the same,' Theo said quietly to Angela as he stood in front of her. He didn't intend to compliment her although she looked attractive. She was wearing a white jump suit embroidered with lace which was sculptured around the breasts. It had delicate shoulder straps but otherwise her shoulders were bare so she had draped a jacket over her arm. The trouser legs were slightly flared and fell just above some high-heeled sandals. It was an expensive outfit but Theo was concentrating on her face which did look the same, albeit with a few creases around the eyes and, perhaps, she was supporting a little more foundation.

'So do you Theo,' Angela replied. 'I'm glad you haven't suffered.' It was a careless remark and she bit her lip as she said it. She meant he appeared well looked after. He hadn't physically suffered, as much as she feared, given his time in prison and years behind the iron curtain.

'I'm going to have a look around town,' Ian interrupted. I'll see you later.'

Theo and Angela mumbled something in reply and Ian headed off into the throng of tourists marching up and down the streets.

Theo had found a small restaurant where they made wood-fired pizzas. The doorway was made to look like the entrance to a cave and the whole interior décor was designed to give the appearance of a grotto. It wasn't expensive but he was a parish priest so he did not want to appear extravagant. In a strange way it also picked up from where they had left off. As students, a dinner at a pizzeria was a real treat.

They were shown to a small table and Angela sat down with her back to the wall which was adorned with vines hanging from the ceiling and a softly lit lamp. Theo sat opposite and the waiter wandered over to him.

'To drink?' the waiter asked.

After checking with Angela, Theo ordered two glasses of the house red. The waiter returned promptly and opened a fresh bottle of wine from which he filled two glasses and then placed the bottle on the table along with a jug of water packed with thick cubes of ice.

'We didn't order the bottle,' Theo protested.

'Just drink what you want and we will see at the end,' the waiter said dismissively as he walked away leaving the bottle on the table.

'I wasn't sure you would agree to see me after I left you at the border,' Angela said hesitantly.

Theo looked into her eyes. He was surprised she could think he did anything other than love her. 'That was never a problem for me. I was glad you got away,' he said gently.

'I felt bad that I ran.'

'Don't be silly. What else could you do? You couldn't have saved me and it's better that one of us got away.'

'That's big of you to say so when you must have suffered at the hands of the Stasi. Did they treat you very badly?' She asked sympathetically.

'They beat me up a bit and chipped all these teeth,' Theo said smiling and turning the side of his face towards her so she could see the damage as he lifted his upper lip with one finger. 'And I suffered a detached retina to the right eye which still bothers me sometimes.'

Angela winced.

'But it was the psychological torture which was worse. They try to disorientate you. Take away all your reference points, so you're floundering like a fish on a riverbank. Then, when you are completely exhausted, they start on your emotions. For instance, they said you had a lover.'

There was an awkward silence as they both looked at each other and then Theo continued, almost out of kindness, as she didn't know what to say.

'But that was true, wasn't it?' There was just a hint of accusation in his voice.

'I was going to tell you when we got to the West,' Angela said, her face reddening.

'And that makes it better?'

The waiter suddenly appeared and just looked at them, holding his pad and pencil at the ready. He had obviously seen too many tourists to maintain any semblance of warmth. Angela grasped the menu and rushed to choose. Theo just said:

'I'll have the pepperoni pizza and a tomato salad,' in a way which indicated the choice of food was not of great significance.

'I'll have the pizza quattro formaggi and a green salad, please,' Angela said, handing the menu back to the waiter.

Angela looked down at the table and slid her hand over to Theo's. She held it as though she was comforting someone. Theo pulled away. It was too symbolic of their relationship. Close but never lovers.

'I can understand you will be asking yourself why?' she said.

'Not anymore,' Theo replied. 'You never said you loved me. You can't force someone to love you. It's a magical thing and if it's not there, it's not there.'

'You can't go out with someone for three years without feeling something,' Angela pleaded. 'It was just I wanted a career and you wanted to settle down.'

'I would have gone along with anything you wanted. You know that.' There was no bitterness in his voice. Theo had come to terms with it all and Angela could see she was losing the argument.

'Can you forgive me?' she said, batting her eyelids.

Theo sighed. He didn't want to think about the past.

'If you love someone, you don't hold grudges,' he said.

'Love cancels any desire for recrimination. It was sad for me but, perhaps, it just wasn't meant to be.'

Angela suddenly realised there was another unresolved question.

'Anyway, how did the Stasi know my situation?'

'Maybe your husband works for them,' Theo replied sardonically. 'It's funny how Ian got attacked when he came to collect my watch.'

'I didn't know that!' Angela exclaimed. 'What happened?'

'He went to a pub, after he left you, and two men tried to get my watch off him.'

'And?'

'And he fought them off but it was a dangerous situation for him and Sophie.'

Angela looked both concerned and puzzled.

'I don't know why you would think Aidan was involved?'

'Because the only people who knew Ian was collecting the watch were you and your husband, unless you told someone else, of course?'

Angela thought for a moment.

'No, I didn't tell anyone other than Aidan.'

'There you are,' Theo said, gesturing by opening his right palm as though to say, "case closed."

During this tete-a-tete, Ian was wandering the streets of Rome, looking up at the buildings and soaking up the atmosphere when suddenly he walked straight into a woman or was it the other way around? Either way, it was a head on collision and she collapsed flat on to the pavement. Ian dropped to his knees.

'Are you okay?' he asked anxiously.

She opened her eyes and tried to sit up. 'I'm okay, I think,' she said, in an attractive Italian accent.

Ian helped her sit up and noticed her long brown gently curled hair which was almost waist length.

'Just get your breath back for a second,' he said.

People started staring and crowding around.

'Can you stand?' Ian asked.

'I think so,' she said grasping on to Ian as he helped her to her feet.

'I'm so terribly sorry. I just didn't see you.'

'That's okay, but can we just sit down for a while,' she glanced at some street tables in front of a trattoria, 'until I get my strength back?'

'Of course,' Ian said helping her to a chair. 'Would you like a glass of water?'

'I think I need something a little stronger,' she said smiling.

For just a second, Ian thought that a little strange. She said it almost flirtatiously and she had a beautiful smile.

'Of course. What would you like?'

'I will have a grappa please.'

Ian beckoned a waiter and gave their order. He had

automatically matched her although he was not used to drinking spirits.

It was only then that Ian really noticed how beautiful she was. Her face was perfectly symmetrical, with a long, fine nose and brown eyes and eyebrows. Her skin tone was bronzed and her lips full, highlighted by a caramel-coloured lipstick.

'I'm sorry, I don't know your name; I'm Ian.' He held out his hand a little awkwardly like an Englishman abroad, not knowing quite how to behave.

'I'm Fi,' she replied shaking his hand as though she was picking something up.

'Oh, is that short for Fiona?'

'No. My full name is Fiorella,' she said laughing.

'What a beautiful name,' Ian said feeling a bit stupid at his earlier assumption and hoping he didn't sound corny. 'In fact, I'm finding everything about Italy beautiful.'

Fiorella smiled at him. 'It means little flower,' she said playfully.

Ian was nervous. He had never been in the presence of anyone quite so overtly stunning. Everything about her seemed perfect as he assimilated her hands, her nails, her clothes. She was wearing a little black silky dress with sparkling shoulder straps stitched with diamond like stones. It hugged her figure and fell just above the knee. She had a matching bracelet and a small black handbag but everything else was bare. Her arms and shoulders, her legs, all bare but her skin was all the same tone and unblemished. She looked like a model.

The drinks arrived and Ian felt the rasping warmth at the back of his throat as he took his first sip of the Italian brandy. Fiorella seemed to drink it more naturally.

'Would you like something to eat?' Ian asked, suddenly realising he was hungry.

'That would be nice,' Fiorella responded with a smile. She recommended a local pasta dish called cacio e pepe which she explained consisted of grated Pecorino Romano cheese and black pepper served with spaghetti and, in a spirit of exuberance, Ian ordered a bottle of Ripasso della Valpolicella.

Even the way she ate her pasta was attractive. She sat straight backed with her left arm bent at the elbow, resting gently on the table, her fingers playing with her hair whilst her right arm formed a mirror image but, with a fork in her hand, she carefully twisted small circles of spaghetti into little parcels and then placed them inside her mouth without disturbing her lipstick.

Ian was talking rapidly, nervously trying to impress, and Fiorella was laughing in all the right places. She kept caressing his arm when he rested it on the table and started calling him *Tesoro* which, he understood, was a term of endearment similar to *darling*. Then she said she was cold and goose-bumps appeared on her arms. Ian stood up and placed his jacket over her shoulders and then, hailing a waiter, he ordered two espressos. He knew he had drunk too much but he wanted to prolong their encounter for as long as possible. Eventually though he had to suggest they depart.

'Well, I suppose I'd better get back to my hotel,' Ian said reluctantly. 'Can I walk you anywhere?'

'Is your hotel far?' Fiorella asked.

Ian was surprised by the question. 'No, it's just around the corner.'

'Can I come with you? I am hoping that you might have a sweater or something I could borrow to go home in? I can't keep your jacket and I have 30-minutes on the bus.'

'Of course,' Ian said, somewhat relieved that her request made sense.

They walked back towards the hotel, Ian feeling too awkward to offer her his arm but Fiorella grabbed it and linked hers through, holding on tightly as though she needed to steady herself.

They entered the foyer of the D'Inghilterra and a concierge in striped trousers and a long black jacket eyed them up carefully.

'We're just popping up to the room to get something,' Ian said clumsily.

Fiorella was still holding on to Ian's arm as they entered the room and she stumbled on to the bed pulling Ian with her. Ian took it as a fall and was about to lift himself off when she put her arms around his neck and paused for a second as she looked into his eyes; then she kissed him. Ian responded automatically. It was what was expected of a man but it felt wrong. It felt wet and her mouth felt too open. It wasn't the same as kissing Sophie. Ian pulled back suddenly.

'Sorry, I just need to use the bathroom,' he said, quickly fleeing from the bedroom and shutting the bathroom door behind him.

He looked in the mirror wondering what to do. He was in too deep. It had all happened too quickly. He wanted Sophie. He knew what was expected of him and didn't think he would be able to oblige.

He splashed cold water on his face and took a deep breath as he opened the bathroom door. He had to bring this encounter to an end. Suddenly, he stopped in his tracks. Fiorella wasn't on the bed. His eyes darted around the room. It was empty. Fiorella had vanished.

Ian sank onto the bed and sighed with relief. His jacket was lying on the floor and he automatically picked it up and started to empty the pockets. He put his wallet on the bedside table and then, from the other inside pocket, he removed his passport and placed it next to the wallet. Then he checked the right-hand-side pocket. It was empty. Quickly, he checked the left. That was empty too. He slumped back on the bed as the penny dropped. The watch had gone.

Chapter Thirteen

The next morning Ian joined Angela for breakfast in the basement dining room of the D'Inghilterra. The lack of natural light reflected his dark mood as Ian felt thick-headed from the night before and a little bit foolish.

'Aren't the frescos lovely?' Angela commented as Ian sat down opposite her. He lifted his head to look at some faded paintings on the back wall near the stairs, which he had just walked down, not noticing them.

'Yes,' he replied distractedly, wondering what all the fuss was about. Granted, they were ancient but that was about all that could be said for them.

Ian ordered coffee and then helped himself to some scrambled eggs and a couple of strips of back bacon. Angela had already started a yoghurt and nut concoction.

'How did you get on last night?' She asked.

'It was interesting,' Ian said, wondering how to answer. 'How about you?'

'I'm not sure what to say really.' Angela paused and looked at Ian. 'I don't know what I was expecting.' She paused again, wanting to avoid anything too personal. She also had something more pressing on her mind.

'Theo said you were attacked after you visited me in Dublin and he said he thought my husband must have been involved?'

'Yes, two thugs tried to get the watch off me but, luckily, I got the better of them. The strange thing is, though, only you and your husband knew that I had the watch. Furthermore, on the way to Hogans, we saw your husband coming out of a phone box which seems a little odd given that you will have a telephone in the house.'

Angela was looking puzzled. 'None of this makes any sense to me. I can't understand why or how he would be involved.'

'It doesn't make any sense to me either,' Ian replied.

'I will certainly ask him about it. As you say, only he and I knew about it and I didn't tell anyone else,' Angela said to reassure him of her integrity, before continuing: 'unless, of course, you were being followed?'

'Maybe I was, but whoever followed me still must have known I was visiting you to collect the watch.'

Angela made an "mmm" sound as Ian looked up from his food. 'Anyway, I think I've fulfilled the initial brief you gave me, but now Theo and I have embarked on a journey to dig up the past, and whatever it is we are on to, someone doesn't want us to find it.'

'But why would Aidan be involved?' she pleaded again.

'I don't know but as this story unfolds maybe we will find out,' Ian said, as he stood, folded his napkin and headed back to his room.

Whilst Ian was brushing his teeth, prior to meeting up with Theo, Simon Black was getting out of a taxi at the Vatican. Father Jacob greeted him and walked him though the grandeur of the palace to a reception room decorated in the Rococo style. Monsignor Demarco Marchetti entered the room and held out his hand so that Black could kiss the ring on his finger. Black was aware that this was heavily symbolic, marking Demarco's seniority but he went along with it reluctantly. They sat down on gilt-edged chairs beside a low rectangular coffee table.

'I have the watch,' Demarco said pulling it triumphantly from his pocket and handing it to Black as though he needed to verify what he was saying.

Black took it in his hand but barely looked at it.

'What now?' he asked.

'Now we lock it away and hope we hear no more about it for another 40 years or more, by which time, hopefully, it will be history.'

'Isn't that called burying your head in the sand?' Black said slightly desperately, as he lacked the time for pleasantries.

'No, it's called perspective. As a British Ambassador to the Vatican once said: "the Vatican reckons in centuries and plans for eternity." We are only just addressing the Inquisition!' Demarco declared, laughing out loud. 'By the time this becomes public no one will care.'

Black turned the watch over in his hand and opened the back. He read the inscription. Nothing struck him as particularly significant.

'Aren't you forgetting something?' he asked rhetorically. 'We were originally told by Schulz that the watch contained the secret combination to open a safe deposit box and I can see there is a serial number on it. You correctly pointed out that safety deposit boxes are opened with keys, but the watch must have some significance. However, my point is, Schulz was meant to secure the watch before Hoffmann and Sutherland got their hands on it, but they have had possession of it for several weeks. Whatever the mystery is, they may have already solved it.'

Demarco looked pensive. 'Good point, but they only arrived in Rome yesterday afternoon, after the banks had closed. If they have solved the puzzle, they won't have had time to do anything about it.'

'So shouldn't we have them followed?' Black persisted, his voice revealing his anxiety. He needed a big win to save his career and he didn't really want to rely on Schulz to achieve it.

Demarco thought his response interesting. He obviously had no back-up. British power was waning but surely MI6 had some resources available in Rome? Unless, of course, Black was on a frolic of his own.

'I think we have done all we can, in good conscience,' Demarco said. 'After all we're a church not a secret organisation.' Black wasn't sure if Demarco was being intentionally sarcastic or not. Demarco continued: 'I think the watch is more likely to be evidential. Let Schulz follow them and we'll see what happens.' He stood up and gave Black his hand and Black departed, for once, not feeling like he was in the driver's seat.

'Do you not think Black has a point?' Father Jacob asked.

'No, I think he is missing the point,' Demarco replied opening a cigarette box and helping himself to what he considered was a well-deserved treat. The Catholic Church prohibited many things but tobacco was not one of them.

'I don't understand,' Father Jacob replied.

'The watch is stamped with a swastika and it has a serial number. That means it was made for someone in the party and Lange & Sohne will know who. That is what I meant when I said the watch was evidential. It links someone to something. Check with Lange & Sohne and let me know what they say.'

Father Jacob scurried away to do as instructed although he already had a good idea, of course, to whom the watch had belonged. He would be happy for the secrets to remain buried but, like Black, he was worried that Hoffman and Sutherland might already be on to something and he had a better idea than Demarco of what that something might be. He was also vexed that Demarco had realised the significance of the serial number. That was clever of him.

I could always pretend that Lange didn't have the relevant records, he thought to himself, as he opened the back of the watch to make a note of the serial number. He put it back in his pocket. No, that was too risky. If Demarco checked, his game would be up.

Ian had agreed to meet Theo at 9.30am at Caffe Greco on Via Condotti close to the Spanish Steps. As the oldest coffee bar in Rome, it was a living museum with memorabilia on the walls and celebrities at the tables. As such, it was more Ian's sort of place than Theo's but he wasn't averse to a little extravagance.

A red Ferrari Testarossa was parked outside the café and a group of young men had gathered around it, so, at first, Ian didn't see Theo. Ian stopped to admire the car. It was very low to the ground with huge air ducts to the side and massive tyres. Ian was just speculating how well it would hold the road and how old fashioned it made his E-Type look when Theo stepped forward.

'Your next car Ian?' he asked teasingly.

'I wish!' Ian replied, but then he hung his head and said: 'I'm afraid I've got a confession to make. I bumped into a lady last night, literally, and we got a little drunk. One thing led to another, and I'm afraid she stole your watch.' Ian spared him the gory details but made it clear he had fallen for a honey trap.

'It's of no importance. We have the keys now,' Theo reassured him.

'But it was your father's. It's a family heirloom.'

'It's a possession. Don't worry about it,' Theo said firmly in a way which made Ian believe the subject was closed.

They agreed on two espressos to pass time until the bank opened, but as they had just had breakfast, they lined up at the bar rather than taking a seat at a table.

The café was busy but in the far corner Ian noticed a young lady sat with an older man at one of the tables. The man had his back to Ian but although the lady was not fully facing him, he could see her face. He merely glanced at her and turned away but then he looked back as she seemed familiar. Her hair was brushed back off her face and tied in a pony tail and she wore a white round-necked cable-knit sweater over blue jeans. She had used little make-up and she was talking in an animated fashion, gesticulating as she did so. Ian noticed she had a sprinkling of freckles on the bridge of her nose and cheekbones.

Ian tapped Theo violently on the arm.

'That's her,' he whispered loudly. 'That's her. It's Fiorella. She's got freckles!' Ian was particularly shocked by the freckles. They seemed to symbolise how foolish he was to have been taken in and the fact that nothing he saw last night was not for real.

'Shall I go and confront her? And ask for the watch back?'

'No, it will be long gone by now,' Theo said, realising

that she would not have wanted it for herself. 'We have more pressing things to do now, Ian. I know it is a sore point for you but let's keep our eyes on the prize. Drink up and we'll go to the bank.'

They consulted a map and headed for Via del Corso, marking themselves out as tourists as they rolled their heads looking for landmarks amongst the tall buildings and walking, open map in hand.

Something made Ian stop and look behind just as Wolfgang Richter darted into the doorway of an expensive jewellers. The guy carried some serious muscle and looked, somehow, out of place. Ian wouldn't have noticed anything if Richter hadn't moved so quickly. It was that which attracted his attention. Ian had a vague feeling he had seen him before but he wasn't sure. Maybe he was one of those guards that stands in the doorways of expensive shops, Ian mused, although he wasn't wearing a suit.

They continued to the bank and walked up the steps into the marble banking hall. It was impressive; designed to inspire confidence with the expression of wealth.

'You need private banking,' a lady at the welcome desk explained as she picked up a telephone. Presently, they were joined by a banking clerk who took them through to a secure area where the deposit boxes were kept. You could just see their frontages like a stack of shoe boxes in a shoe shop.

'Four-digit number?' he asked.

'1135,' Theo replied.

'Key?'

Theo handed over the keyring.

'I just need one. One to remove the box. The other is for you to open the box.'

The bank clerk took one key off the keyring and asked them to wait but he remained in their line of sight. He returned straight away with the safety deposit box and he showed them into a small room.

'When you are ready,' the clerk said as he left, which Ian assumed meant "come and get me when you are ready to leave."

Ian and Theo sat at a small table and Theo opened the box. There was a large number of Swiss Francs, some documents folded in two and tied with ribbon, like a barrister's brief, and an envelope with the name "Renate" handwritten on the outside.

'Renate?' Ian asked.

'My mother,' Theo replied, tearing open the envelope.

'Is it okay to read it?'

'Yes, my mother won't mind. I will have been a child when it was written and it could contain essential information.'

Ian could see it was several pages long and Theo started reading out loud, translating from the German for Ian's benefit.

'Dear Nette, that's short for Renate,' he said. His voice was quiet and reverential.

'You've worked out the coded message in the deck watch – well done! I'm sorry to have been so obtuse but it is far too risky to be open about these things.

I was hoping to see you and Theo soon but I am afraid I may soon be meeting my maker. The doctor says I have liver atrophy but I think I have been poisoned.' Theo put the letter down momentarily.

'So, someone killed him,' he said, looking at Ian. He continued reading.

'I suffered two days of sickness and diarrhoea which left me feeling very weak but then I thought I was starting to recover. However, my skin has turned yellow and, clearly, I have jaundice.

I am not in any pain but I am unable to eat and I feel I am burning up inside.

I am so sorry to be putting you through this but if you can see it through, justice will be done and my death will not be in vain.

You know how upset I have been at work recently, sending money to Argentina so Nazi refugees can start new lives with false identities. I was reassured they were only foot soldiers following orders and that they deserved a second chance but this was not always the case.'

Theo's voice was getting deeper as he read and he spoke slowly as he tried to assimilate the contents.

'Last week I was asked to assist with the urgent transfer of a prisoner of war from Rimini to Britain. It was well known that he had been in the Galician SS. However, he is Austrian and he is guilty of the most heinous of crimes. In 1944 he was in command of a group of soldiers that entered the village of Huta Pieniacka, a Polish self-defence outpost, occupied by partisans. It was also a shelter for Jews. The partisans had shot two of his men and by way of reprisal, he ordered his soldiers to round up the residents of the village and lock them in a barn. He then had the barn set on fire and if anyone tried to escape, they were shot.'

Again, Theo put down the letter and just looked at Ian in disbelief.

'Several hundred inhabitants were killed. Women, children; they all died.' Theo was shaking his head as he carried on reading.

'But one young Jewish boy never went into the barn. He hid in some bushes and escaped under the cover of darkness. Good,' Theo said.

'He discarded his Jewish armband and made it to Poland where he acquired a new identity. He couldn't go back to his homeland and he didn't want to go to Germany so he headed for Italy, with many other refugees, where he hoped to make contact with the Allies. Then, one day, as he waited for a train at Bolzano, he recognised the man from his nightmares. The Nazi commander from the Galician SS was there in front of him. His name is Ernst Junger.'

Ian was listening intently, his mouth slightly open but Theo didn't notice as he carried on.

'The boy, who is now sixteen, went to the police but, at first, they said he must be mistaken and then they said he had no evidence. In the meantime, Ernst Junger is quickly being transferred, as part of the Ukrainian contingent, to Britain.'

'It's beyond belief,' Ian said shaking his head. Theo, on the other hand had speeded up. He wanted to find out what else the letter revealed.

'You may wonder why anyone would want to help him? I did. It works like this:

⅄ The Roman Catholic Church invested substantial sums of money into the Third Reich in the 1930s which, at the time, was quite legitimate. Most of these investments are now worthless and the Church is anxious to re-build its wealth.

⅄ One such investment was in an Austrian company with a factory in the Tyrolean city of Bolzano. It has some special paint formulae of military and strategic importance. For the last twelve months, Junger has worked for this company, using a false identity.

⅄ Originally, this company was owned by a Jewish family but it was sequestrated by the Nazis at the start of the War. The owners died in a concentration camp.

⅄ A British company, called BCI, wanted to obtain the patents and know-how and they were willing to pay for them. This would enable the Church to crystallise its investment so they struck a deal.

⅄ BCI paid the money into a Swiss Bank account and the Swiss Bank transferred it to the Vatican Bank. This cannot be traced because Vatican City is a Sovereign State and the Vatican Bank is unregulated.

⅄ The Vatican Bank intended to lodge the patents and formulae with the Swiss Bank which in turn would pass them on to BCI.

⅄ When the money was received from the Swiss Bank, I diverted it to my own account and I never transferred the documents. Both are in this safety deposit box.

⅄ Junger is needed by BCI to run the business. He knows the formulae, and he has the technical expertise to manufacture the paints.

⅄ I dare not give this information to the British Secret Intelligence Service because I think they may be complicit and if they are involved the Americans will know all about it too, so my idea was to hand the information over to Israeli intelligence.

⅄ I did not see why the Church should profit from its ill-gotten gains which is why I diverted the money to my own account. I thought we would need it to make a fresh start and perhaps, when we were on our feet again, I would try to trace the surviving relatives of the company's founders.

⅄ I would like you to pass this information on to Simon Wiesenthal. I think he will make sure it gets into the right hands. Please also give him the deck watch. When Junger asked for help, he had destroyed all his true identity papers in case he was arrested. He produced the watch, however, because he knew its purchase could be traced back to him and it was sort of proof that he was who he claimed to be.

⅄ You might think I should have taken my concerns to the Church first. I did, and it was suggested I should meet with Junger to see if he could allay my fears. Everyone has a right to give their side of the story. So, we met for dinner which was cooked by his Ukrainian assistant called Kolesnik. We ate veal and mushroom stew and Kolesnik made a big show of the tiny pfifferlinge mushrooms which were in season. However, I believe I was poisoned and my symptoms match those caused by eating the death cap mushroom. Perhaps he mixed some in?

I am sorry it has come to this, my darling. I had such high hopes for our future. I know you will look after Theo, so all I will say is, every time you hug him, give him a hug from me.

May God keep you safe,
Werner'

Theo's eyes were full of tears but he immediately started looking through the other documents. There were only about a dozen pages, some with sketches on, others with lists of numbers.

'Are you okay?' Ian asked, desperate to tell him

something.

'How much money is there?' Theo replied, as he continued sifting through the papers. Ian could see he was angry so he started counting.

'About 250,000 Swiss Francs, I think.'

They both looked at each other not quite knowing what to say. Eventually, Theo broke the silence.

'I'm going to leave the money here, go to the Vatican and confront them with the documents. I will say they have to start putting their house in order or I will shine a light on that which they want to keep hidden. Then I'm going to send the documents to Simon Wiesenthal, like my father asked; and I will say if he can trace the heirs of the company, I will send them the money. If he can find Ernst Junger, if he's still alive, well,' his voice trailed off and he shook his head.

'He is,' Ian said quietly.

'Is what?'

'He is still alive. He lives in Leeds.'

Chapter Fourteen

Ian and Theo walked out of the front doors of the bank into the winter sunlight and stopped at the top of the steps whilst their eyes readjusted. Theo had a determined look in his eyes and was about to descend the steps when Ian put his arm across his chest to stop him.

'You see that man,' Ian said, indicating towards Richter who was standing behind some café tables across the road. 'I'm sure he's following us.'

Theo started to get a grip of his senses. He was upset and raging with anger but he realised he had to deal with this situation logically.

'Okay,' he said. 'Let's split up.'

Ian looked at the map. 'If you head for the Vatican via the Pantheon and Piazza Navona and then cross the Tiber at Ponte Umberto, I'll go to the Spanish Steps and cross the river at Ponte Cavour. We can then meet up in the Piazza San Pietro.'

'Good idea, but here, take this letter,' Theo replied. 'If anything happens to me, give it my mother.'

Ian trotted down the steps and set off in a north-easterly direction towards the Spanish Steps and Theo headed south. Ian glanced behind and saw Richter turn away, towards a line of parked Vespas. Theo saw this and quickly delivered a prayer for Ian's safety. He then hurried at a fast-walking pace in the direction of the Pantheon.

What neither of them had noticed was that there was a second man with Richter. Schulz was desperate. Following his meeting with Demarco, Black had made it clear to Schulz that he had to deliver or there was no deal. Black needed the information to save his career and Schulz needed it to save his life, so he started following Theo, leaving a discrete distance between them.

Schulz had a gun, brought in via a diplomatic bag, but he didn't intend to discharge it. His plan was to confront Theo at the first quiet spot and demand he hand over whatever it was he had just collected from the bank. Richter was meant to take a similar approach with Ian. The difference was Richter was trained in combat.

Almost like a sixth sense, Theo felt Schulz's stare and quickened his pace. He was breathing heavily and starting to perspire. Schulz too was out of breath; more so than Theo because he had a smoker's lungs.

Their concentration was on each other so neither noticed that they were both being followed by a third man.

Ernest Boyes knew what it was like to be on the run. The freezing cold and constant hunger. Always looking over your shoulder and having to use false identities. He wasn't going down that route again. He liked his position of standing in England. He enjoyed his wealth and power and he was determined not to let Theo ruin everything. He had worked too hard for that. Of course, he was in his early seventies but he was a hard man. He couldn't leave this to his hot-headed son Hayden or contract it out. He was a firm believer in the exhortation: *if you want something doing properly, do it yourself,* so he too tracked Theo but he was only a little way behind him and on the other side of the road to Schulz.

Ian broke into a gentle jog. The real chase hadn't started yet but he was subconsciously trying to put some distance between himself and Richter. Ian turned down Via Borgognona and Richter accelerated. Ian heard the change in tone of the engine and saw the pale-yellow scooter indicate right as Richter closed the gap. It was now clear; the chase was on.

Theo had made it to the Piazza della Rotonda. The magnificence of the Pantheon was in front of him; the vertical architecture of the pillars at the front, lifting his eyes heavenwards. A gypsy woman was sat on the steps of the fountain in front of him; begging. She gave him a gapped-toothed smile which was so endearing he dropped some coins in her bowl before pressing on. Schulz was on his tail crossing Piazza Capranica. Theo had to make a decision which way to go. He glanced at his map and took the road on the left-hand side of the Pantheon; Via della Minerva. It looked a slightly more mainstream route to Piazza Navona but he didn't have much time to think. Schulz followed. Boyes took Via della Rotonda, down the right-hand side of the Pantheon. Now, Theo was out of sight. Boyes had to rely on his instinct. Theo turned right at the end of the street. Boyes turned left. They were now at the back of the Pantheon on Pizza di Santa Chiara. No one was nearby. It was a back street and they met at the narrowest point in the centre. Theo looked surprised as he rounded the corner and they came head-to-head. He stopped abruptly and then he gasped as Boyes slid the blade under his top rib and into the base of his heart.

Boyes felt Theo's weight sag on to the knife. He felt heavy. He held him up for a split second.

'Your father was nothing more than a common thief,' he said, staring closely into Theo's eyes. Then he pulled away the knife.

Theo fell on his knees and then collapsed backwards. Boyes grabbed the papers tied with the ribbon. He turned and walked calmly away back down Via della Rotonda as Schulz rounded the corner.

He was observed by the gypsy woman because he walked not like a tourist but with determination in his step. She observed the drop of blood as it fell from the knife hidden up his sleeve and she observed him as he discreetly let his arm sail over a dustbin as he walked past.

Theo lay on the ground, his life-blood draining away from him just as Schulz rounded the corner. He bent down and nestled Theo's head. It was almost tender, but Schulz was the last person Theo wanted by his side as his soul moved from one world to the next.

'The file?' Schulz asked anxiously.

Theo shook his head.

'Who did this?'

Theo's eyes were rolling. He knew this was the end and much as he disliked Schulz, he knew he was the only person to whom he could pass information. He had his suspicions but he wasn't sure. He couldn't condemn a man on a whim. It was in God's hands now.

'Don't know,' he mumbled.

He was straining to say something. 'Tell Ian,' he said but then some blood bubbled out of his mouth and he started choking. He was hanging on with every ounce of strength he could muster. 'Tell Ian – be happy,' and then his chin sank and his eyes closed.

Ian lengthened his stride and started running properly. Not into a sprint but his normal running pace. He turned left up Via Mario de' Fiori and smiled to himself. It was one-way and Ian was running up it the wrong way. Not a problem for Ian but, hopefully, it would be for Richter. He glanced back as Richter reached the crossroads. For a second it looked like Richter was going to follow but there was too much traffic heading straight for him and he went straight-on, further along Via Borgognona. Ian turned right, on to Via dei Condotti. He could see the Barcaccia

Fountain and Spanish Steps in front of him but Richter was zooming in from his right, the Vespa making a high-pitched squeal as Richter maintained full throttle.

Ian shot up the first flight of steps towards the Obelisco Sallustiano. It was effortless as the muscle memory simply referred back to the training at Studley Deer Park. Richter pointed the Vespa towards the steps and lifted his body from the seat but the first two steps were too steep and he was thrown forward, stumbling, although just able to keep on his feet.

Ian paused. It was time to stop running and with the fortification of the Trinita dei Monti church behind him, Ian turned to face his fate.

Richter ran straight into him, grabbing Ian around the waist and knocking him to the ground but Ian used the momentum to his advantage and putting his feet on Richter's stomach he somersaulted backwards, throwing Richter behind him. Ian scrambled round and jabbed his elbow into Richter's face, but Richter rolled sideways and got to his feet.

They both stared at each other as a crowd started to form around them. Richter launched himself at Ian again as Ian took the boxer's stance. The man was made of granite and this time he whipped Ian's legs from beneath him. Ian landed hard on the base of his back and felt a shoot of pain travel up his spine, but there was no time to hesitate. As Richter came towards him, Ian kicked out and caught

Richter in the chin with the flat of his heel. Again, Richter was able to brush it off.

The crowd was getting bigger and Ian became aware of the noise as some people looked on in shock and others looked around for a policeman. Both men got to their feet.

For a third time Richter charged Ian but this time Ian managed to stay standing and kept hold until both men lost their balance and started rolling down the steps in a close embrace. They wrestled with each other, neither achieving a winning blow, until they reached the fountain.

Richter pushed Ian into the water, forcing him in, with his hands pushing against Ian's chest. The power of the man was overwhelming. He had more weight than Ian and he knew how to use it. He pushed Ian under water and held him there. Ian knew he had to do something quickly because he was out of breath but he couldn't overcome the weight bearing down on him. He was desperate to breathe. He could feel the strength draining from his body. He was running out of time.

Against all his instincts, he relaxed. He emptied his lungs, blowing out bubbles as he did so, releasing the pressure in his chest. He sank lower in the water and his body went limp. Richter thought he was finished. He softened his grip and as he did so, Ian jettisoned out of the water like a rocket, head-butting Richter on the nose. Richter stumbled backwards and instantly Ian sucked the air back into his lungs and with all his might threw a punch hitting Richter again on the nose. The nose split and blood poured from Richter's face as he fell backwards onto the stone floor of the square.

Ian leapt out of the fountain. He knew he had the advantage and he knew he had to finish Richter off whilst he had the chance. Richter had half stood up, looking dazed, his body shaped like a question mark. Again, Ian hit him on the nose and he staggered but didn't fall. And again, Ian hit him. Each time in the same place, spreading his nose across the side of his face. Then Ian heard the sound of a whistle and two policemen running towards him from the top of the steps. He took one last look at Richter who was sitting on the ground, his face covered in blood, and he started to run.

It wasn't comfortable. Ian was already gasping for breath, his wet clothes sticking to him and his body pumping with adrenalin, but he knew what to do. He had to recover whilst running. He took deep breaths; as deep as he could. Pulling the oxygen into his lungs and expelling the carbon dioxide as quickly as he could. He ran the way he came, back down Via dei Condotti but then he realised he had to lose the police so he followed his nose, turning right, then left, then right, then left until he reached some gardens with a circular building and a sign saying Mausoleo di Augusto. He could see the river and Ponte Cavour behind the building so he slowed to a trot, then a fast walk as he joined the traffic on the bridge.

There was no one behind him as he crossed Piazza Cavour and seeing some trees in front of him, he went into Paco della Mole Adriana and sat down with his back against the trunk of a tree to gather his thoughts.

Ian's clothes were soaking wet and clinging to his body although they were starting to dry in the late morning sun. He checked himself over. He was okay. There were some cuts and bruises but otherwise he seemed to have come through this unscathed.

Ian stood up and walked the short distance to St Peter's Basilica. His Cleverley shoes squelched as they expelled the excess water. He thought they would be ruined but when he looked down at them, they looked fine. He mingled amongst the crowds in Piazza San Pietro but Theo was nowhere to be seen. That's funny, Ian thought, he should have made it here before me. Ian looked at his Rolex. The black leather strap was ruined but the watch was still working. It was 11.30am. Ian waited until noon and then started to worry. He decided to head back along the route he had suggested to Theo. He made it to Piazza Navona and considered getting a drink but realising the state he was in, decided against it. He looked at his map and exited the piazza from the south end and headed towards the back of the Pantheon. Ian didn't realise it was the back; it just looked like the most direct route. As he approached, he saw a police car, people milling around and then an ambulance. Ian hesitated thinking he might be a wanted man but then banked on the police not having a sufficient description to identify him. Anyway, these guys looked busy.

Ian moved closer. A body was being put on a stretcher. They started wheeling it towards the ambulance. Suddenly, Ian felt sick. A feeling of dread came over him. He pushed through the crowd to the policemen wheeling the stretcher.

'I think I know this person,' he blurted out.

The policemen stopped and eyed him up and down. It was only then that Ian remembered what a state he was in; wet and filthy. One policeman pulled back the blanket covering Theo's face.

'You know him?'

'Yes,' Ian gulped.

The policeman covered Theo's face again and allowed his colleague to load the ambulance. Then he looked at Ian suspiciously and grabbing his arm he pushed him in the direction of a police car.

'You're coming with us,' he said.

Chapter Fifteen

Simon Black was staying at the Hilton, not far from the airport. He didn't like Rome. Too crowded. Too many tourists and too many petty thieves, so he didn't want to be in the centre. However, he didn't want to see Schulz on home ground so he agreed to meet him at Café Greco, where all the tourists go. It would be busy but that would make it safe.

Schulz entered the café with a worried expression and he still had a film of sweat on his forehead from his earlier excursions. He smelt even worse than usual. He plonked himself down at the table Black had chosen. Black was facing the entrance so Schulz had his back towards it.

Black was drinking tea. He liked to be different and Schulz grunted 'espresso' at the waiter.

'Hoffman's been killed,' Schulz started. 'Stabbed outside the Pantheon.'

'Unfortunate,' Black replied showing no emotion.

'Don't know who did it.' Schulz was talking in staccato sentences and still seemed a little out of breath. 'It happened in the few seconds he was out of my sight.'

'And Sutherland? Didn't you have a man on him?'

203

Black almost seemed concerned.

Schulz nodded and said: 'Richter. They got into a fight and Sutherland got the upper hand, apparently.' Black smiled. 'He's in police custody now. I was still watching when he arrived at the crime scene and he identified the body so the police took him away for questioning. Richter is getting the next flight out of here before they identify him as the other man brawling on the Spanish Steps.'

'So, what about the information? I assume you followed them to the bank?'

'Hoffman and Sutherland split up when they left the bank so I'm pretty sure they found what they were looking for but I asked Hoffman for the file and he shook his head. There was nothing on him so I reckon his killer took it.'

'Well, I'm afraid that leaves nothing for me to work with,' Black said winding up the conversation. 'We will just have to say *auf wiedersehen*.'

'What about my defection?' Schulz asked anxiously.

'We'll have to forget about that. I've nothing to offer my superiors,' Black said trying to make it appear that it was out of his hands.

'But I've more to offer. Other information I can provide.'

'The Cold War's over now. Well almost,' Black said correcting himself. 'We're all moving on.'

'So that's it?'

'I'm afraid so, old boy. It's back to Germany for you,'

he said condescendingly. 'But stay in touch.'

Ian gave only minimal information to the police. He said Theo was a friend and they had agreed to meet at the Pantheon. When he didn't show Ian walked around the back and seeing a body feared the worst. Ian was able to give the name and address of Theo's mother which the police were grateful for as they needed the next of kin for the legal procedures and, as to his wet and dirty appearance, Ian said he had been knocked into the Trevi Fountain by a mass of Japanese tourists. The gypsy woman had directed them towards the murder weapon so the police took Ian's contact details and let him go.

Up to this point Ian had been working on adrenalin but now the shock started to set in. He was making his way back to the D'Inghilterra but suddenly became cold and started shaking. He knew he would have to break the news to Angela but decided to have a hot bath first. Before he went upstairs, however, he pulled the letter from Werner out of his back pocket. It was wet and the ink had run but it was just about legible. He passed it to the receptionist and asked for three copies.

'I fell in a fountain,' he said by way of explanation.

Back in warm dry clothes, Ian asked to meet Angela in her bedroom. He arrived carrying two glasses of brandy.

Angela noticed his pale colour and instantly knew something was wrong.

'What is it?' she asked.

Ian handed her a brandy and she sat on the bed. Ian sat beside her and, as gently as he could, he told her that Theo had been murdered.

Angela burst into tears burying her face in her hands. So many emotions were going through her mind. She was glad she had seen Theo before he died but it hadn't been a perfect reunion although he harboured no grudge. Now he was gone and she had been told her husband was a spy. Was he involved in all this? And Theo had been murdered! Why? What was going on?

Ian said what he could. Explained what he could. Angela was flying back to Dublin tomorrow morning and there wasn't a lot more he could do. He did make one promise, however. He said he would make sure that all the information he had found its way to the right people.

Ian went back to his room and thought about things carefully. Whatever the merits of the case, the money belonged to the Vatican and Ian felt he could use it as a lever. He made a call, asked for the VIS and said he had some money to hand over. An hour or so later he received a call back and an offer of an appointment to meet with Monseigneur Demarco Marchetti the following morning.

Demarco was a scary looking guy. He had an ability to make people feel they had done something wrong with a constant air of disapproval but Ian was not easily intimidated. In fact, Ian was gestating a growing sense of anger and that anger was preparing him to challenge.

Demarco held out his hand, horizontally. Ian thought that odd but gave it the best shake he could in the circumstances. Demarco frowned.

They sat in the same setting as Black had done a couple of days earlier.

'You know Theo Hoffman is dead,' Ian commenced.

Demarco wasn't falling for that trap. In fact, he had heard of the murder from Black and was feeling decidedly awkward over it, but he feigned ignorance. Consequently, after painting the background Ian continued:

'We visited a bank before he died and accessed a safe deposit box utilised by his father.' Ian paused.

Demarco raised his eyebrows and eventually said: 'And?'

'Amongst other things it contained 250,000 Swiss Francs.' Ian pulled the keys out of his pocket and dangled them in front of Demarco. 'I think, nominally, the money belongs to the Church.'

Demarco was responding slowly and carefully.

'And what else did you find?'

'Details of things the Church got up to in the aftermath of the War.'

Demarco was a cold fish and he wasn't going to rise to the bait.

'And where is that information now?'

'Theo was bringing it to you but the file was taken by his murderer.'

Demarco sighed gently. The first tell-tale sign he had inadvertently allowed himself, but Ian didn't miss it. If it was with relief, it didn't last long.

'The good news is, Werner Hoffman summarised everything in a letter,' Ian said with a hint of sarcasm as he pulled an envelope out of his jacket pocket and flapped it in front of Demarco.

Demarco breathed in deeply through his nose and then out again. 'You can't judge the past by present standards. You need to have been there at the time.'

Ian rubbed his hand across his mouth and looked pensive. 'It looks dubious through any lens to me.'

'You must understand, Communism was consuming Central Europe, threatening the very survival of the Church.' Ian had Demarco on the back foot.

'So that justifies the smuggling of Nazi war criminals out of Europe to the safety of Latin America?'

'They were refugees. Prisoners of war and missing persons; foot soldiers, mainly. Yes, some were freedom fighters.'

'Like Eichmann?'

'He got his comeuppance,' Demarco snarled.

'And money had nothing to do with it? You didn't put the Vatican Bank at the disposal of the Nazis so they could transfer their wealth out of Europe? Most of it stolen from their victims.'

'The Church lost a lot of money as a result of the War.

We had a lot of ground to recover. Anyway, you can't have got all that from a letter.' Demarco was starting to recover himself and wanted to close down the meeting.

'I would have thought,' Ian said standing up, 'that the Church, in its struggle against Communism, would have put its faith in God. It seems to me, it chose espionage instead.'

Demarco shifted uncomfortably in his chair.

'You can have the money,' Ian said as he tossed the keys across the table. 'I'm not sure who it really belongs to but I expect you to find out.'

'And the letter?' Demarco asked.

'It's going to Simon Wiesenthal. I can imagine what he will do with it but you should have a bit of time to put your house in order.' Ian turned away and then looked back over his shoulder. 'Because you know what they say.'

'What?' Demarco snapped as he too stood up.

Ian turned back to face him. 'All roads lead to Rome.'

When Ian got back to the hotel the concierge said a gentleman was waiting for him in the bar so instead of going upstairs, Ian turned left into the brightly lit room with its red wall paper and white ceiling and large mirrors and paintings on the walls. Immediately he saw Simon Black sat in a corner on a brown studded-leather bench seat with a small glass topped mahogany table in front of him.

'I could have guessed you would be behind this,' Ian said abruptly.

'Not at all,' Black replied indicating that Ian should take a seat. 'I suspect our interests are aligned.'

Ian sat on a studded-leather chair opposite Black and a waiter came over to take Ian's order. Black was drinking a negroni and Ian asked for some water.

'So, what interest does MI6 have in this sorry matter?' Black could see that Ian was angry.

'I'm sorry for the death of your friend,' Black said showing a rare expression of empathy. 'It must have come as quite a shock.'

Ian started to garner his thoughts.

'I was ambushed in Dublin, followed and attacked in Rome and now Theo has been murdered and I've no idea who is behind it all. The Church seems to have been involved in some shady dealings but I can't believe they would be behind a murder, so I repeat my question. What has MI6 got to do with all this?'

'You know I can't discuss that but let me reassure you that in this, we are innocent bystanders.'

'So, what is it you want from me?'

'MI6 has been given information indicating that a Nazi war criminal may be residing in the UK. I don't know his identity but I believe you might?'

'And if I did, what would you do with that information?'

'Not much, probably,' Black shrugged. 'Observe him; consider his position. We might make a move against him but I can't promise anything. I suppose it depends on the circumstances under which he entered the country.'

'And what would the information be worth?'

Black eyed Ian carefully. 'I know you're not asking for money?'

Ian shook his head. 'I want to know who is behind this. I want justice for Theo.'

Black took a deep breath.

'The information we have originates from the Stasi. From an individual who wants to defect. It is the Stasi who have been following you. This individual was with Theo as he died. His last words were, "tell Ian – be happy."'

Black had such a way with words. He knew how to unsettle and Ian was knocked off his stride.

'That's not always easy,' Ian replied with a heavy sigh.

'They were his last words.'

'Did this individual kill him?'

'I don't think so because if he had, he would have the information. He's desperate to defect and, as he couldn't deliver, we've turned down his application. Presumably, Theo's killer has the information now but I'm hoping you know the details too? You were at the bank together.'

Ian sat back and looked withdrawn. He put his hands behind his head and stared at the ceiling for a moment; then he pulled the envelope from his jacket pocket and took out a copy of the letter. He slid it across the glass-topped table.

'This will tell you all you need to know.' Ian then stood up, took a last swig of his water and walked out of the bar.

Ian wanted to get back to England as soon as possible but he had one last job to do before he left and that was to see Theo's mother. She was flying in the next morning to deal with the formal arrangements. He wasn't looking forward to it.

Ian met Renate at the airport. She stood out in the crowd as she came through customs; a solitary figure in black. Black trousers over black ankle boots, a black blouse and black leather jacket. Her face looked drawn and haggard.

The airport was not the best place to talk but they needed to talk and to delay matters until they got into town would be awkward.

'Would you like a coffee?' Ian asked.

'Yes,' she replied.

They found a quiet corner in an airport café and Ian went to the counter and gave their order. A black coffee for Renate and a cappuccino for himself.

Renate was holding it together but she was probably still in shock. Ian explained some of the background and gave her the original letter and a copy.

Renate read the first page and looked up at Ian.

'They have both died. Not just Werner but Theo too.'

Ian nodded sadly and Renate carried on reading.

'So, I have a job to do,' Renate said as she put the letter down and took a sip of her coffee. 'I will get this information to Simon Wiesenthal and ask him to pass it on to Israeli intelligence.'

Again, Ian simply nodded.

'Where is the watch?'

'I'm afraid I allowed it to be stolen,' Ian said guiltily.

'And the money?'

'I gave the keys to the safe deposit box to the Vatican. I felt it was their problem and up to them to get it to the rightful owners.'

'Good. I don't want it – it's blood money.'

'For the third time Ian nodded and said: 'I agree. It's best to approach this with clean hands.'

Renate looked at him in a way only a mother can. 'Many people in this have dirty hands,' she said, 'and I will find every one of them.'

Chapter Sixteen

It was late when Ian got back to Studley Roger and the cottage was cold and empty. Sky was with Nell and Sophie was still in Munich. Apparently, she had given up her job at the University. Ian had vaguely hoped they would both be there to welcome him but he was now dealing with the harsh realities of life and it wasn't about to get any easier.

He got into work the next morning and there were hushed whispers. He could tell people were talking behind his back but he had no idea what they were saying. The jungle drums were beating and the sound was ominous.

Eventually, Thompson entered Ian's office and sat on the opposite side of his desk.

'Trees,' he said without any pleasantries or explanation.

Ian looked puzzled and screwed up his face. 'I'm sorry?'

'You should be.'

Again, Ian frowned. 'I'm sorry, I have no idea what you're talking about.'

'Mr and Mrs Trees. Ring any bells?'

'Mr and Mrs Trees, the farmers? I act for them.'

'Yes,' Thompson said in a long drawn out way as

though Ian was being completely stupid.

'What about them?'

'Why don't you tell me. What should you have done?'

'Well, they've just bought some extra farmland.'

'Yes, and how did they pay for it?'

'With a bank loan.'

'And did they buy it in their own names?'

'No, through their farming company.'

'So, what should you have done?' Thompson was labouring every point and suddenly the penny dropped.

'Register the loan at Companies House,' Ian replied.

'And how long have you got to do that?'

'Twenty-one days after completion.'

'Oops. Well, I wonder when that deadline expired?'

'I left my work with Ed to look after.'

'Can't blame him. He has his own work to worry about.'

'So, are you saying we've missed the deadline?'

'You've missed the deadline. We have had to hold our hands up to the clients and the bank and now we have to go to Court to see if we can get a court order to register the loan out of time. It's going to cost us thousands not to mention the embarrassment. You've probably cost us another good client.'

Ian was looking concerned but he knew this was a set-up.

'What do you want me to do?' he asked.

'Go home.'

'What?'

'We want you to go home. Your work has been re-assigned. We'll give you a bit of time whilst you look for another job and still pay your drawings – say for three months.'

'You can't make me do that. What does Hannah say about it?'

'We've had a partners' meeting and the decision was unanimous. You're persona non gratia now.' Thomson stood up. 'Oh, and clear your desk before you leave.'

Ian just sat there in total and utter shock. He didn't move for several minutes but then grabbed a brown cardboard box, threw all his belongings into it and headed for the carpark.

The E-type was parked at the back of the office and as Ian filled the boot, Ed slipped out of the staff entrance looking very anxious and clearly not wanting to be seen, as he kept looking over his shoulder. He thrust a note into Ian's hand.

'This was put on your desk for me just before you left for Italy and shortly after, I was told to leave your work alone altogether so more senior colleagues could look at it.'

Ian looked at the note. *Do the bare minimum,* it said.

'I'm sorry,' Ed said. 'Most of the staff are on your side.'

'Don't worry about it,' Ian replied as he opened the driver's door. 'I'm not giving up without a fight.'

Ian had formulated some ideas with Sean Blake before

Christmas but he had not been intending to implement them so soon and there was also the shock to deal with. It is one thing thinking about something but quite different emotions come into play when you have to put it into practice.

Ian got home, grabbed Sky and went for a walk. He didn't feel up to going for a run but he just kept walking, choosing the longer route whenever an option was presented. Through Studley Park and Fountains Abbey, then on to the village of Markington. From there, Ian walked to Markenfield Hall and across the fields to Whitcliffe Lane and back to Studley Roger. He had no idea how far he had gone – maybe eight miles – but he felt better for it.

Back at the cottage, Ian started preparing something to eat, for himself and Sky, when he noticed there was a message on the answer phone from Angela so he gave her a call.

'I've separated from Aidan,' she said. 'He's worked for the Stasi all this time. I've suddenly realised I don't really know him. I'm going to sell the business and move to England. I want to invest in property and I thought you could help me.'

Ian expressed his reluctance and told her about his problems at Ryders. Angela listened carefully and after a brief silence said, 'Can't you see, this is an opportunity? I am willing to back you financially if you want to set up your own firm and we could run a sort of partnership with the property development. I need someone I can trust, and I hold you in very high regard.'

Ian's mind was working overtime. 'What I need is a letter from your bankers saying I have financial backing to the tune of £500,000. I won't need the money but the letter will be useful. Then, when I have sorted out the issues at Ryders, we can move our other plans forward. Do you think you can arrange that for me?'

'I will certainly try,' Angela replied.

The next morning Ian telephoned Thompson.

'I've thought about what you said and I am willing to stay at home, if that is what the partners wish, but I'm not prepared to give up my partnership so please make sure the accounts department continues to pay my drawings; indefinitely.'

There was a long silence whilst Thompson's mind did somersaults.

'What do you mean you're not prepared to give up your partnership? You can't just take your drawings for nothing,' he said at last.

'I think you will find I can, although I'm willing to work. You can't expel me, Mark. The only way you can get rid of me is to dissolve the partnership.'

Ian could sense Thompson squirming at the other end of the line.

'I'll get back to you,' Thompson said slamming down

the phone.

When he did, it was to suggest a meeting at the offices later in the week at midday.

'Just come to reception and I will escort you to the board room,' Thompson said. Ian didn't like that. They were treating him like a leper.

High noon arrived and in actual fact it was Sarah who took Ian to the board room, in silence. The room was empty and Ian remained standing, looking towards the door. Ronnie Roberts was the first to enter. He looked embarrassed but was too polite to do anything other than shake hands and say, 'How are you?'

Ian said he was fine, then in single file, the other partners piled in. Once everyone was sat down, Thompson started the proceedings.

'I was a bit taken aback by your bluff yesterday but we still want to sort this out amicably,' Thompson said feigning reasonableness. 'Take your time to find another job and we will continue to pay you for, say, three to six months. We'll prepare a deed of retirement from the partnership and ask you to sign an election that the partnership continues for the remaining partners, for tax purposes. I think that's pretty generous?'

'Bluff?' Ian replied.

'Well, you can't just hang on forever.'

'I like being a lawyer in Harrogate,' Ian replied, 'and Ryders is the best firm in Harrogate, so I intend to stay unless, of course, you dissolve the partnership.'

'You've got a nerve,' Steve Fell interjected.

Hannah glared at him. 'Quiet,' she said. Ian could see her mind racing. She realised these negotiations were sensitive and she didn't want them wrecked by someone being overly aggressive.

'What is the advantage of making us dissolve the partnership? It has adverse tax consequences for all of us. You will just be making an awkward situation more difficult,' she said pleading to his sensibilities.

'I don't want to make you dissolve the partnership but it does provide a solution, of sorts,' Ian replied calmly.

'How so?' Julie Short asked, intervening.

'Have a look at section 39 of the Partnership Act,' Ian responded. 'My understanding is partnership property is applied in the payment of the debts and liabilities of the firm and then the surplus assets are distributed between the partners; and for that purpose, any partner may apply to the Court to wind up the business and affairs of the partnership.'

'There are no surplus assets,' Thompson retorted. 'Assets and liabilities are about equal.'

'You're forgetting goodwill,' Ian countered.

'Goodwill's not in the accounts,' Thompson argued, but he didn't understand these things as well as Ian.

'That doesn't mean it doesn't exist,' Ian said, slamming the ball straight back into their court.

There was silence for a while as the other participants tried to fathom the implications of what Ian was saying. Eventually, Ronnie Roberts spoke up.

'So, you want us to attribute a value for goodwill and pay you something. Is that what you're saying?'

'Not at all,' Ian replied. 'What I am saying is that on a winding up I will bid myself for the name, *Ryders*. I will bid for the lease. I will bid for the telephone number and all the other assets of the partnership, including work-in-progress. I will then continue in business here. I will keep on all the staff and may ask some of you to join me.'

A wave of disbelief rippled around the table. No one knew how to react. Some were angry and some were thoughtful but no one dared speak as they tried to assimilate what Ian had said.

'How will you finance it? We will outbid you,' Thompson said playing into Ian's hand.

'Perhaps you will,' Ian replied as he opened his file. 'I am quite happy to share with you the value I place on goodwill. I think it is worth around half a million and that is what I am willing to bid.' Ian pulled a letter from Angela's bank from his file and slid it across the table. 'This shows I have the finance in place.'

Ronnie Roberts looked indignant. Fell glared through his pig-like eyes and Thompson was puce. Hannah looked worried. Ian stood up.

'Anyway, I'm sure you have lots to talk about. Give

me a call when you've had time to think about it,' he said as he left the room.

The silence hung over the room like a storm cloud until, eventually, Julie Short spat out the words, 'He's got a cheek,' with venom.

'I wonder which of us he'll ask to join him?' Ronnie said worrying about the next step in his career.

Thompson let his head smash on to the table with a loud bang, then he lifted it up, his face glowing like a burning orb. 'No one will be joining him,' he growled. 'He's not getting his hands on this firm.'

'We could take his money and set up in competition?' Evans suggested.

'And call it something other than Ryders? Over my dead body,' Hannah replied firmly. 'No, we are going to have to think about this very carefully and take some advice. I suggest we resume this meeting later.'

The days passed and then the weeks without Ian hearing anything. His emotions were all over the place. He was still angry about Theo. There was an unresolved murder and Ian hated injustice. Then there was the fantasy of his own situation. He *could* implement his plan. He knew you should never make a threat unless you are prepared to carry it out, but it would be better for him to start his own firm. However, until the situation at Ryders was sorted out, he couldn't make his next move and as time passed, he was losing momentum. He could dissolve the partnership himself, of course, but then there was no turning back; no deal to be done.

Month end came and went so Ian drove into Harrogate to check his bank account. Relief; his drawings had been paid in as usual. They're playing for time, he thought as he walked from the bank to the newsagents. He had decided to go for a coffee at Bettys and buy a newspaper so he didn't look a complete loser sat on his own.

Ian was given a window seat and as he sat looking at the gardens across Montpellier Parade, he thought about Sophie. He missed her and wanted to get her back. He opened the paper and went straight to the business section, as he always did. That's when he stopped and stared at the photograph. It was an image of Ernest Boyes. The headline said he had been arrested in Israel and charged with crimes against humanity.

A waitress came to take Ian's order but he didn't even see her. She had to interrupt him.

'Cappuccino,' he said, distractedly, and then shouted, 'please,' as she turned away.

It said he had been arrested in mysterious circumstances. His yacht was abandoned off the Israeli coast and his lawyers were arguing it had been hijacked in international waters.

'It was,' Ian said out loud just as his coffee arrived.

'Excuse me?' the waitress replied.

'Sorry, I'm miles away. Just ignore me,' Ian said. Then

under his breath he mumbled, 'It's not just the Mounties that always get their man.'

Within a couple of days Thompson was on the phone asking for another meeting but this time it was to be with just him and Hannah and he wanted to hold it at a firm of accountants which acted for Ryders. Robert, their accountant, would chair the meeting. Ian agreed on all counts.

The meeting room in the accountant's office was small, bland and cheaply furnished and the Robert looked uncomfortable. He was being used to make the next step in Thompson's plan look like a necessary part of the procedure and both he and Ian realised this.

'We want to work with you on this Ian, so what we suggest is that Robert carries out an up-to-date valuation including work in progress and bad debts and then he will come up with a formula for goodwill which we will keep off the balance sheet but, in due course, we will make a payment to you reflecting your share in the surplus assets of the business. In the meantime, you find another job and we will pay your drawings until you have got yourself sorted and contra those payments against any monies due from the surplus assets.' Thompson paused to let his offer sink in and then said, 'How does that sound?'

'So, you want me to leave without any prior agreement as to the amount payable or even when it is to be paid? How do you think it sounds?' Ian replied looking at

Thompson with contempt.

'In the circumstances, I think it sounds a very fair offer,' Thompson spat back.

The words *in the circumstances* did it for Ian. He could see Robert wondering what they were. Ian stood up.

'There are no circumstances. Good-bye.'

Hannah stood up quickly. 'Don't leave,' she said anxiously.

'No, I am leaving because there is nothing further to discuss,' and with that Ian left the building. He was, of course, acting; showing he was prepared to walk away, and, by his actions, showing his disgust with the offer but he was in better control than the impression he gave.

Ian started putting plan B into action and that was the setting up of his own firm. He wanted to take Ed and Debbie with him but didn't dare say anything to them in case there was a leak at this crucial time. He got as far as contacting the Law Society to see what the regulatory requirements were but then Hannah telephoned him suggesting just the two of them had lunch the following day.

She chose the Bruce Arms at West Tanfield, a small village just north of Ripon, obviously so they would not be seen by their Harrogate peers but the lunch was painful. She would not tackle the elephant in the room and instead embarked on laboured small talk probing personal matters such as friends and family. Ian let her lead the way as she had asked for the meeting but he was guarded.

Eventually, after coffee, she suggested a walk along the riverbank.

'Your offer of £500,000 equates to about £70,000 per partner,' she said. 'If you push us, we are prepared to dissolve the partnership but rather than do that we will give you £70,000 if you resign and sign an election of continuation for tax purposes. We will give you until close of business on Friday to make up your mind.'

Ian knew you should never accept the first offer but, in this case, she had given him all he wanted. Now he had to appear reluctant and cement the final terms.

'The only reason I will consider accepting is because it would be difficult to manage the work-in-progress of those partners that didn't join me. So, these are my terms: I will set up my own firm and I want to take Ed and Debbie with me and £20,000 worth of work-in-progress. Basically, all my trust files. The remaining £50,000 you pay in cash, by close of business on Friday.'

Hannah stopped and looked at him, the river rumbling in the background.

'Deal,' she said and held out her hand. Ian shook it. They walked a little further, towards their cars, until she stopped and turned to face him.

'Tell me, would you have pulled the trigger?' she asked.

'Without hesitating,' Ian replied.

They continued walking in silence until they reached the carpark.

'You probably need a holiday after all this?' Hannah said sympathetically.

'I think a short break might be in order,' Ian replied.

'Let me guess, The Ritz?'

'No, Munich.'

William Kinread is a solicitor
and company director. He lives
in North Yorkshire with his
wife, son and dog.

Also by William Kinread
Luger.

CPSIA information can be obtained
at www.ICGtesting.com
Printed in the USA
LVHW042138160222
711307LV00018B/1998